Force Protection Delta, Book 1

Charissa Gracyk

Ryland

Published by Charissa Gracyk

© Copyright 2023 by Charissa Gracyk

Edits by Michelle Fewer

Cover by Monique Walton/ moniquewalton515@gmail.com

ISBN: 9798860139916

ASIN: B0CH77YVC4

Dedication

To all of the men and women who sacrifice so much to keep this country safe. My eternal gratitude and respect. You are all the badasses I wish to be.

Force Protection Condition (FPCON) is a Department of Defense (DoD) approved system standardizing DoD's identification of and recommended preventive actions and responses to terrorist threats against U.S. personnel and facilities.

There are five Force Protection Conditions: FPCON Normal, Alpha, Bravo, Charlie and Delta.

FPCON Delta is the highest state of alert and action and references a specific, known threat. In this case, The Agency.

"Be this the whetstone of your sword. Let grief
Convert to anger; blunt not the heart, enrage it."

–MacBeth, William Shakespeare

"If you prick us, do we not bleed? if you tickle us, do we
not laugh? if you poison us, do we not die? and if you
wrong us, shall we not revenge?"

–The Merchant of Venice, William Shakespeare

Chapter One

I'm about to get barreled. Fuck yeah.

Ryland "Rip" Mills knew it was his wave the moment he saw the set rolling in. He was good at reading the waves, knew the ocean like the back of his hand, and this beauty had his name written all over it. The lip feathered briefly in the wind then pitched forward, exploding in a foaming, rushing cloud of water. Everything seemed to move in slow motion as he paddled hard, keeping his chin down, then popped up fast. After a good bottom-turn, he was riding inside the breaking wave, one hand dragging along its silky center.

"Hooyah!" Ryland shouted the Navy cheer as he experienced the ultimate thrill ride. Hell, it was a near-religious experience. Such incredible speed, yet it was totally smooth and eerily quiet inside the tube. A complete paradox and moment of absolute awesomeness.

1

The lip feathered in front of him and he let out another triumphant shout.

Then it was over and he dropped into the ocean. *Best feeling ever.* Maybe even better than sex. Not that he remembered. Hell, thanks to the chaotic schedule of his new job, he hadn't been laid in over six months. There might not be time for dating, but he always made time to surf.

The San Diego sunshine sparkled on the waves as he stepped on the shore, turned and lifted a hand to shield his eyes from the bright glare as he looked back over the surf. Moments later, his friend and teammate rode a wave right into shore and slapped Ryland's hand.

Ryland and Tanner "Mayhem" Stiles weren't members of just any regular squad, and the rules were made clear the first night they met—keep your true identity secret and no fraternizing outside of work.

But that all went out the window the moment Tanner spotted a surfboard hanging out the back of Ryland's Jeep after their first meeting six months earlier. It was a bro-at-first-sight moment and the instant bond turned into a solid friendship.

Would The Agency approve? *Hell no.* But Ryland and Tanner didn't give a flying fuck. What they did could be too heavy sometimes and surfing was one of the ways they let off steam. Sure, they could surf alone, but they needed to be able to make their own decisions, too. Not

2

just mindlessly follow all of the rules that didn't always make sense issued by their mysterious employer.

The Agency, a black ops organization, had recruited six of them for their team. They were mostly former military, or so Ryland assumed, with some international flavor courtesy of Saint who had a very slight accent that Ryland pegged as Russian. Since they weren't supposed to get too personal or even share their real names, he had no idea what anyone's background was for sure.

But the one thing he did know was his team, dubbed Ex Nihilo by their employer, was the best of the best. And they proved it every single time they went out and hunted down their targets.

One-hundred percent success rate.

"That was bitchin'," Tanner exclaimed, slicking his wet blond hair back. "I'm jealous."

Both men were former Navy SEALs and possessed a love for the water that not everyone did. Ryland quickly learned that when it came to his SEAL brothers, it was one extreme or the other. Either a guy enjoyed being wet or they dreaded leaving dry land and bitched every time they had to dip a toe in the water. But, either way, they were highly trained warriors who knew how to operate and excel in any type of situation involving the water.

"Are you going back out?" Ryland asked, shaking his head and sending water droplets flying through the air. He slid a hand through his brown hair lit with golden highlights and the tattoo on his forearm flexed with the movement. The ink, representing DEVGRU's Red Squadron, his special ops SEAL team, consisted of a tomahawk with red and black feathers.

The tattoo hadn't just been the result of a drunken dare. It was his only tat and sacred to him. Although he wasn't opposed to getting more, he'd only do so if there was a significant reason for it. The ink was more than just marking up his body. Like surfing, getting a tattoo was almost a spiritual experience and whatever design he chose next would hold deep meaning.

"Nah. It's going to start getting crowded."

"Good point. Let's go grab some breakfast."

They'd been riding waves since seven and, as the nine o'clock hour snuck up on them, the tourists would start showing up with their umbrellas, coolers and squawking kids. Time to head out. Besides, he was starving.

They loaded their boards into the back of Ryland's Jeep, slipped t-shirts over their heads and flip flops on their feet. He enjoyed living in the laid back beach town and knew Big City life would never be for him. Los Angeles could keep its traffic and smog. He much preferred Coronado's Main Street entertainment and surfside splendor. They hopped inside the Jeep and Ryland headed toward Sunrise Cafe, a local joint a little ways up the road where the food was greasy, cheap and hit the spot.

In less than five minutes, Ryland pulled into a slanted parking space out front, and they ambled inside and sat down in their usual spot on the back patio overlooking the ocean. Ryland couldn't imagine living in a place where he didn't always have an ocean view. He needed the salt, sand and crash of waves like he needed the air in his lungs. It was a part of him—always had been—and was one reason he'd been interested in becoming a SEAL. Just like his dad before him.

"Lemme guess. You boys just finished surfing." Beth grinned as she poured black coffee into their mugs. Their server had worked there long before Ryland started eating there and he had a feeling she'd continue to happily serve plates of bacon and eggs until she retired. She genuinely seemed to love the job and acted like everyone's long-lost mother.

"I got barreled," Ryland said proudly, puffing out his chest.

"Good for you," Beth replied, not impressed in the least. She'd heard all their surf stories. Although they had been known to exaggerate occasionally to keep their tales entertaining, they always found the biggest waves and didn't hesitate to ride them. "The waves are pretty big today."

"You ever wanna learn to surf, Beth, you just let us

know," Tanner told her with a grin.

"I'm sixty-two years old," she announced, "and not looking to land in an early grave much less one of your tubes."

The guys laughed.

"It's never too late," Tanner insisted and Beth shook her head.

"What do you two jokers want to eat?"

"The bacon omelet," Ryland said without looking at the menu. "With extra bacon."

"And I'll have pancakes and sausage."

"Coming right up," Beth said and turned to place their orders.

Tanner leaned forward, forearms pressed against the table, icy blue eyes twinkling. "So, what's up with your new neighbor? You ask her out yet?"

Ryland finished swallowing his sip of coffee as an image of Harper jumped to his mind. He could feel his pulse speed up as he pictured the petite blonde with aqua eyes the color of the Caribbean Sea. She was the first woman to catch his attention in a long time, and his dick wasn't letting him forget it.

"Not yet," Ryland admitted, moving his silverware around. Truth be told, Harper made him nervous.

6

Normally, if he saw a woman he liked, he'd approach her, no problem. But his new neighbor was different and he didn't want to screw it up.

"What're you waiting for? A written invitation?"

"I'm waiting for the right moment."

"What if that never comes?

"Then I guess we never go out."

Tanner snorted. "Just bang her and get it over with."

"Great advice. Thanks," Ryland said dryly and rolled his cobalt blue eyes.

"No problem. That's what I'm here for."

Beth arrived with their breakfast quickly and they thanked her as she set the heaping plates of food in front of them.

"Where do you think we're headed next week?" Tanner asked in a low voice the moment she walked away.

"No clue, but I'm sure we'll find out soon enough." They had a meeting later that afternoon about their next job. The team always met at the same building, which had no address and didn't show up on GPS, in the same unmarked office on the third floor. It was all kept under the radar and Ryland thought it was a bit too mysterious and dramatic. But, hey, they paid him to follow orders, not ask questions.

Ryland took a big bite of his omelet and nearly groaned. In all his 28 years, he'd never found a better bacon omelet than the one served at Sunrise.

Tanner swallowed down some pancakes and eyed Ryland over his fork. "You ever have second thoughts about what we do?" he asked quietly, blue eyes serious.

"Are you asking me if I lose sleep over taking out bad guys? Negative."

"Yeah, me neither."

They grinned at each other. From the moment they met, it was like they recognized they were kindred spirits. Both former Navy SEALs, both loved the ocean and surfing, both the youngest on the team at twenty-eight and both enjoyed the single life, occasionally adding a beach bunny on their arm. They always seemed to be on the same page, totally in sync, and Ryland hadn't had an instant friend like Tanner since he met his buddy Jason on the first day of first grade. But ever since Jason got married and moved north, they didn't have quite as much in common anymore.

The best meal of the day devoured, Ryland drove Tanner back to his apartment. Tanner hopped out, removed his surfboard and slapped a hand against the side of the Jeep. "I'll see you later."

"Yeah, see ya at command central."

Ryland headed back to his apartment complex. It wasn't a big place, but he was a simple guy and didn't need anything fancy. Especially since he traveled so much and didn't spend a lot of time at home, anyway. It was near the ocean and made the time he spent there worth the lack of square footage.

After pulling into his parking spot, Ryland turned the Jeep off, grabbed his board, placed it under his arm, and walked over to his mailbox. He hadn't checked it in a few days, and he didn't usually get much more than credit card offers with insanely high interest rates. *They should save their postage,* he thought, because Ryland didn't need a credit card. He made good money working for The Agency and paid cash for everything. His bank account was healthy and he didn't lose any sleep over what he did to earn that money.

"Hi." A feminine voice behind him caught his attention and Ryland turned as the object of his fantasies moved closer.

Harper Grant. Small, blonde and with a mouth made for kissing. And every single time Ryland was close enough to see the light dusting of freckles across her nose, he wanted to kiss each one.

He swallowed and couldn't stop the goofy grin that curved his lips up. "Hey, Harper." *Just be cool,* the little voice in his head instructed. What was it about her that

9

made him lose his mind a little?

"How are you?"

"Good." His normal cool wavered. *Shit. Say something…anything…*

She nodded to his board. "Catch any waves?"

"Yeah, I got shacked."

Her delicate brow scrunched, clearly confused by his surf lingo.

"It's, ah, when you ride the inside of the wave."

"Oh, right." She gave him what she thought was the shaka sign, but instead was the symbol for headbanging rock-n-rollers. "Hang loose, brah."

Ryland chuckled. "Close, but not quite right." With a crooked smile, he reached out, took her soft hand in his and bent her index finger down. "There you go."

His words came out husky and their gazes locked, the air between them instantly igniting. Ryland couldn't deny the zing of awareness that passed through him when he touched her. His attention dipped to her glossy lips. Hell, he wanted to taste them more than he wanted anything else.

Pulling in a steadying breath, he released her hand and raked his fingers through his wild, sun-streaked hair. It was too long on top, but he liked it that way. And, unlike the Navy, The Agency didn't care how long he let it grow. Before Ryland lost his nerve yet again, he blurted out, "Would you like to go out sometime?"

So much for waiting for the perfect moment.

There was no missing the way her aqua eyes lit up. "I'd like that."

He nodded, his usual confidence returning. "Great. There's this place not too far away called Driftwood. They have the best food."

"Oh, I passed by there the other day. It's right on the beach."

"I'd take you tonight, but I have a work meeting that could go late. So how about tomorrow evening?"

"Sure." She tilted her head, studying him. "What do you do for work?"

He hesitated briefly. "I'm former military and now work for a government agency."

Her eyebrows shot straight up and when he didn't offer any more information, she flashed him an adorable, half-smile. "Like the FBI? Are you a spy or something?"

The FBI had agents; the CIA had spies. And Harper had an abundance of artless charm.

But Ryland needed to shut down any and all conversation about what he did for a living. Because as far as the world knew, The Agency didn't exist. And it was up to him to keep it that way by not giving away any details about what he actually did for a living.

"Nah. Nothing that exciting." Okay, so a bit of a lie, but the less she knew, the better. Flipping the conversation, Ryland said, "You just moved to San Diego, right?"

"Almost three weeks ago."

"What brought you here?"

He could've sworn a dark look flashed over her pretty face before she said, "My sister lives here and she recently bought a restaurant that she's renovating. I offered to help her and she accepted. I've always liked San Diego, and L.A. lost its charm about a year ago."

Ryland propped his arm on top of the row of mailboxes and leaned closer. "Why's that?"

Her gaze dipped to the tattoo on his forearm. "The people just aren't very nice. Unless, of course, you can do something for them. Then they're your best friend." The dry tone in her voice spoke volumes.

"Phonies?"

She nodded. "It's okay. I'd much rather be down here. It seems more real."

"I think so." He straightened up and glanced down

at the large Casio G-Shock watch on his wrist. "Well, welcome to paradise. I should get going, though. Can't be late or the boss won't be happy."

"See you tomorrow then?"

"Definitely. I'll come over at six to get you."

"Apartment two-twelve."

"Two-twelve," he repeated. *Roger that, sweetheart.* Ryland gave her another smile, and his gaze trailed hungrily along her curves as he watched her walk. For being so small, she had plenty of them. Mouth watering, eyes glued to the sway of her hips and rounded ass, he mentally groaned.

What would it be like being with someone like Harper? He'd dated his fair share of women, but no one like her. She possessed a feminine elegance that had been missing from his latest line-up of beach bunnies and party girls. Harper was definitely a relationship kind of girl and not just some casual hook-up.

Looking forward to their date, Ryland headed over to his apartment, whistling a low tune. It had been a long time since he'd been out on an actual date. *Years.* Usually, he'd meet a woman at the bar or on the beach. They'd hang out and he always kept things light and fun. Anytime a woman tried getting serious, he'd hit the brakes, explaining that his job didn't allow it.

And that was the truth. Before separating from the Navy last year, he'd spent most of his time deployed halfway across the world. The workload never lightened and being a SEAL meant constant training. His time off was precious and he didn't waste it. Any spare moment was spent doing what he loved—surfing, swimming, hiking. He craved the outdoors and that connection to nature. No orders to follow, no rules to abide by. Just the wide-open beyond, ready to be explored and appreciated. It was freeing for his mind and necessary for his soul.

In all honesty, he also didn't make time for dating. Pleasing a woman was a lot of effort and he was still young. At twenty-eight, he had no desire to get married or start a family any time soon. Hell, his own family had never been the greatest example of marital bliss either. His dad had been a workaholic who'd devoted his life to the Navy. That caused a lot of stress, among other things, and his parents separated when he was thirteen. He and his older sister Addison barely saw him once a year after the split. Then he died during a mission when Ryland was eighteen and his mom passed not long after.

Ryland had always been fascinated by the stories his dad told him about being a Navy SEAL. After he learned his dad died, Ryland signed up with the Navy, determined to follow in his father's footsteps. Maybe it was his way of trying to keep his dad's spirit alive. Maybe he wanted the challenge. Whatever it was, Ryland pushed himself harder than he ever had before. The day he received his Trident pin, he knew his dad was watching from somewhere, and he was so damn proud. Even though Nathan "Cross" Mills hadn't been physically present, Ryland had heard his voice in his head, congratulating him with a resounding, "Hooyah!"

Reaching into the neckline of his t-shirt, he fingered the silver chain and cross hanging around his neck. It was the only physical thing he had from his father and he'd never taken it off. Not even throughout all of his missions.

Normally, Ryland didn't spend a lot of time thinking about his dysfunctional family. It bothered him that he and Addison barely talked since losing their parents. But whenever they did, the siblings inevitably got into an argument about her life choices. His sister had a lot going on and he didn't approve of any of it. He missed her, though. Addie was strong, sassy and the most intelligent woman he'd ever known. That was half the problem—she was far too smart for her own good and that led her into constant trouble.

At least the Navy had kept Ryland busy and out of the endless shenanigans Addie was always neck-deep in. But once he separated from the military, he floundered a bit, feeling like he'd lost his purpose. In a moment of weakness, he very briefly considered joining the "family" business. Luckily, The Agency recruited him fairly quickly and he turned his energy toward them.

Now he once again found himself wondering if it

was time for another change. After mere weeks of knowing she existed, Harper was making him think about things a little differently. Like maybe he was spending too much time running around the world chasing down bad guys. Maybe there was more to life.

Or maybe it had just been too damn long since he'd been laid and he needed to chill the fuck out and stop reading into everything.

Propping his surfboard in the corner, Ryland grinned. He had a date with Harper Grant and he wasn't about to fuck it up.

Chapter Two

Harper calmly closed the door to her apartment then squealed and broke out into a happy dance. He finally asked her out! With a sigh, she dropped onto the couch, feeling very much like a melting stick of butter.

Ryland did that to her. Every time she ran into him, her heart picked up its pace until it was galloping inside her chest. With his wild brown hair highlighted with golden streaks, cobalt blue eyes and sun-bronzed skin, he was delicious in the most achingly beautiful kind of way. Plus, she'd been lucky enough to catch a glimpse of him shirtless and the sight had stunned her into immobility, driving every last breath from her lungs. She could've bounced quarters off those flat, ridged abs. Even now, her fingers itched to skim along his tanned skin.

They had talked briefly in passing, but it never

amounted to much and she began to worry that he had a girlfriend. Because let's face it, the man was a golden god of epic proportion. There was also the worst-case scenario—he simply wasn't attracted to her. Although he'd been polite and chatted her up for a few, breath-stealing minutes, he hadn't hinted at anything beyond a casual, friendly neighborly greeting.

Until today.

Her lower belly tightened at the idea of spending some quality time with him tomorrow night. Beyond knowing he liked to surf, drove a Jeep and was former military, she knew practically nothing about him. She wondered what branch he was in. Being so close to Coronado and the base, her gut said a Navy SEAL. Plus it was written all over his ever-present surfboard and sun-kissed face—the man loved the water and being outside.

Blowing out a soft breath, Harper felt giddy, excited and nervous all rolled into one. *Reel it in,* she told herself. It was just dinner. Plus, meeting a man was low on her priority list right now. She'd promised herself she was going to step back from the dating scene and take some much-needed me-time.

Well, so much for that. But, hell, after all she'd been through up in Los Angeles the past year, she deserved something good.

Despite vowing to remain single for a while, there's no way she could've said no to Ryland. *Gah.* The guy was too gorgeous, and the attraction she felt every time they crossed paths was too difficult to write off or ignore.

After leaving her LaLa Land nightmare behind, Harper came down to San Diego to work on her withering self-esteem and improve her non-existent finances. Helping her sister Savannah renovate and open the restaurant she recently purchased should have been enough to occupy her time, keep her busy and focused on herself. But now she couldn't stop thinking about Ryland Mills. And talk about knowing nothing about him, the only reason she knew his last name was because she'd caught a glimpse of it on his mail. *You're such a stalker.*

With a soft sigh, Harper forced herself to shut down the tantalizing images of her sun-bronzed neighbor and got up to feed Betty.

"Are you hungry?" Harper asked, walking over to the small tank sitting on the kitchen bar. Betty, her Betta fish, swam all around and Harper could've sworn she was smiling at her. Well, smiling as much as a fish can.

Also known as a Siamese Fighting Fish, Betty had been a sad mess when Harper first laid eyes on her a few weeks ago. She hadn't realized just how much fight Betty had left in her when she decided to bring her home. Relegated to a dimly lit shelf at the back of a local pet store, the poor thing was floating in the smallest bowl Harper had ever seen. Her coloring faded, fins tattered, the sickly-looking thing had appeared so depressed.

Harper had watched her float lethargically for a few minutes, started to cry and then dug out the last of her cash to pay the $3.29 scrawled on the sale sticker taped to Betty's pitiful little home.

After two weeks in a new tank in Harper's bright apartment, Betty's dull pink scales had turned into a vibrant red, her energy was restored, and bright blue appeared on her fins. Dropping some food pellets into the tank, Harper watched the tough, little fish eat for a few minutes and realized she was the perfect example of resilience.

Sometimes you had to fight through the darkness and hard things, trusting that once you came out on the other end, things would get brighter again. Sure, it required you to dig deep, find your inner strength and take matters into your own hands, but it didn't allow shitty ex-boyfriends named Patrick and pet stores with crappy owners to get the last word.

Harper didn't believe in dwelling on her failures, though, and she was determined to put her past behind her and not let it affect her future.

Grabbing her purse and keys, Harper locked up. She was bursting at the seams and needed to share her exciting news with someone. And by someone, she meant Savannah—her constant confidante and biggest support system.

It didn't take long to reach the restaurant just off

Main Street on Coronado Island. Harper knew once her sister had the place up and running, it would attract the Navy boys. No doubt about it.

Parking her Prius out front, she walked up to the front door and knocked. A minute later, Savannah appeared, grinning at her a little too widely through the grimy glass. She unlocked the door and with a flourish of her hand, said, "Welcome to the shithole. I hope you're here to help because I'm about to have a nervous breakdown."

"Oh, no. What's going on?" Harper walked inside and winced. The place looked worse than she remembered.

"The inspector came by today. Apparently, there are previous violations on file that I didn't know about. And the bathrooms aren't ADA compliant. So that, in addition to new fixtures, means widening the doorways so they're wheelchair accessible. Oh, and they found asbestos in the windows, so those all have to be removed, remediated and replaced." Savannah ran a frustrated hand through her blonde waves that looked so much like Harper's. "All these costs are adding up so fast and I'm starting to panic. Maybe I should cut my losses and get out while I still can."

"No! Opening your own place is your dream. And I'm here to help, remember? We'll figure it out, even if we have to get more loans."

"No bank in their right mind is going to lend me any more money."

Harper looked down, knowing they wouldn't give her a penny, either. But she had to stay positive for her sister. "You've got this, Savvy. I know it." Harper grabbed her sister and pulled her in for a hug.

Savannah was two years older and Harper's best friend in the whole world. Even though they were like night and day, they understood each other on every level. While Savvy, ever the pragmatic one, wrote the list of cons, Harper encouraged her to buy the place with a solid list of pros. Somehow, she convinced her realist sister to follow her dreams.

Shit, I hope I didn't steer her wrong. Look what happened to me after I tried following my dreams.

Squashing those thoughts down, Harper released her sister and stepped back, eyeing the plastic covered tables, buckets, rags, paint cans and array of tools scattered across the floor. "What can I help you with?"

"I was just sanding the bar down so I can stain it." She swiped up a piece of sandpaper and offered it to Harper. "Care to join me? It promises hours of endless fun."

"Sure."

The sisters sat down on stools and started sanding

the scarred bartop. For a few minutes, they focused on the task at hand and the sound and motion was a good distraction from the current situation. Neither wanted the bar to fail before it ever had the chance to begin.

"So, enough with my bad news," Savannah finally said. "Why're you glowing?"

Harper pressed her lips together and tried not to smile, but she couldn't contain it. "Oh, it's nothing. Just going out with Ryland tomorrow night." Though she tried to downplay it, Harper was unable to stop grinning.

Savannah paused sanding, looked over at her sister and frowned. "Your neighbor? I thought you were taking a break from dating."

"Technically, he lives a few doors down. And Ryland is nothing like Patrick," she assured her, setting the sandpaper aside. "I know you're concerned and that's your job as a big sister, but I'm also nothing like the girl I was with him. I learned a lot. I'm not making the same mistakes again."

Savannah arched a dark brow. "Part of the reason you left L.A. was because of your breakup. If that happens again—"

"I'm not leaving here. Promise."

"I hope not. You just got here."

"You're all I have, Savvy. Los Angeles may have

chewed me up and spit me out, but San Diego feels like home."

"Still though." She let out a sigh. "You've only been here a few weeks and you're just getting back on your feet."

Just getting back on her feet was a bit of an understatement. After their parents died, the memories had been suffocating and the sisters decided to leave their small town in Ohio and head West. To establish new memories by pursuing their dreams. After all, Charlie Grant, their father, had always encouraged the girls to chase after their hearts' desires.

Harper decided that meant Hollywood. Memories of hours sitting beside her dad on the couch, watching all the old movies on Turner Classic, inspired her to reach for the thrill she imagined surrounded that lifestyle. She admired the glamorous starlets who flitted across the screen. Reveled in the tales of found fame and fortune prevalent in the behind the scenes documentaries they binged.

She never had serious intentions of moving to L.A. For her, acting was a fun hobby. Something to extend the joy of theater she shared with her dad. She'd done all the school musicals and local theater productions she could to satisfy her acting bug. And her parents were always there with the loudest applause and the biggest bouquets of flowers on opening night.

But then, her parents passed. And she and Savannah were forced to sit down to discuss their futures. Futures that no longer included or carried the support of two of the most important people in their lives. In that moment of grief, the sting from the dramatic backhand of reality still fresh on her cheek, Harper decided to do it. To move to Los Angeles all by herself and try to break into the entertainment business.

In memory of her dad.

Little did she know it would turn out to be the worst decision of her life. She wasn't sure what she'd expected, but falling flat on her face wasn't it. Lucky for her, in addition to his love of classic movies, she'd also inherited her dad's positive nature. She might fall, but she also knew how to bounce. And that rebound brought her back to her sister. So, as much as it hurt, it wasn't the end of her world. Again.

"Promise to take it slow, okay?"

"I will. I'm just going to dinner with him. That's it."

"What do you know about this guy, anyway?"

"He's former military—"

"Probably a SEAL. They're everywhere."

"—and now he works for the government."

"Doing what?"

"I don't know. When I asked, he got kind of cagey and turned the question back around on me."

"Maybe he's a spy."

"That's what I said!"

Savannah gave her a cautious smile then started sanding the bar again. Peeking sideways, she asked, "Is he cute?"

"He's a tall, bronzed god with 6-pack abs and dark blue eyes."

"You think everyone is tall," Savannah said with a chuckle.

"Everyone *is* tall, but he's extra tall." At barely 5'3", Harper felt like a munchkin standing next to Ryland. A full head and shoulders above her, he towered over her. The guy had to be at least 6'2". She squeezed her thighs together. Tall guys always turned her on and Ryland was no different.

"I thought you swore off men," Savannah reminded her innocently.

She had. After Patrick kicked her out, she didn't have anywhere to go and wound up living in her car for a month. Harper supposed that was partly her fault for being so damn stubborn. She could've come down to San Diego sooner. But, in her mind, leaving L.A. meant giving up on acting, and she hated the idea of letting her dad down. Everything she'd been doing was for him.

It was the main reason she'd stayed so long and tried so hard. She wanted to make him proud. Imagined him smiling down on her and bragging to everyone, "That's my Harpsichord," his special nickname for her.

Truthfully, she never liked much about the city. It was too big, too crowded and too dirty. People weren't friendly, especially in the business, and the amount of competition she faced for one stupid job was overwhelming.

Harper had doled out far too much money during the last year pursuing a dream which, when she really dug down deep and acknowledged it, was barely hers. The monthly rent for her apartment was outrageous, her car insurance doubled, gas prices tripled and then there were all the costs associated with acting—headshots, classes, meetings over lunch or coffee. The entire fiasco turned out to be a money pit and the little cash she'd gotten after her parents died burned up fast. Once it was gone, she felt like a fool. Another Hollywood failure who was no closer to success than she'd been when she first moved there.

And then the guy she'd been dating, the one who invited her to live with him after she lost her apartment, broke up with her. He'd kicked her to the curb so fast her head had spun. Of course, she'd been hurt. Not devastated about losing him, but more so by the way he'd done it…the things he'd said…

"I'm just not attracted to you anymore, Harper."

His cold words still echoed through her head. *Wow.* Talk about a punch to the gut. Her ego was still bruised.

"You have to admit, what little spark there was burned out a while ago."

She'd only been dating the actor wannabe for three months, but the fact he'd started dating some D-list actress the day after dumping Harper still stung.

He'd kicked Harper out and moved Chloe in all in less than twenty-four hours.

As if that wasn't bad enough, his parting words were an added low blow. It wasn't enough that he made her feel unwanted by him; he made her question things that would make her unwanted by anyone.

"And, c'mon, the sex was only okay. We both know it. But you'll get better."

True, she didn't have much experience and Patrick was only the second guy she'd slept with, but his callous remark was beyond insulting. It was hurtful. He made it sound like it was all her fault she'd never had an orgasm with him. Like she was bad in bed. She certainly remembered him having orgasms, so it couldn't have been that bad. *Jerk.*

Harper's first sexual partner barely counted. Less first-time bliss, more drunken college fiasco. He'd been so wasted the experience barely lasted a few minutes. Just a few grunts, pumps and done. Not one romantic memory about that encounter and she'd been in no hurry to do it again. But Patrick had been nice, cute. He approached her and started chatting while in the waiting room during a casting session. L.A. was a lonely place and she enjoyed their conversation.

At twenty-five, she was not innocent or naive, but she lacked experience and was curious, so she agreed to go out with him. Their relationship wasn't very exciting and he certainly never gave her butterflies, but she had to give herself credit for trying.

"It's over, Harper. You're going to have to find someone else to mooch off of because I'm done playing Sugar Daddy."

His cruel words ringing in her ears, she'd packed what few possessions she had left—she'd already sold most of them—and moved into her Prius. It was the lowest point of her life. But she pushed herself to still go out on auditions, lived on ninety-nine cent Del Tacos, washed up in the park bathroom and refused to call her sister for money.

A month later, without a single acting job to her credit, and down to her last twenty dollars, she decided to leave L.A., drive to San Diego with her tail between her legs, and hope Savannah would hire her to work at the restaurant.

Of course, her sister had welcomed her with open arms—just like she knew she would—and helped her start to get back on her feet. The entire humiliating experience was behind her now, but it was a lesson she couldn't allow herself to forget.

So, yeah, she'd definitely sworn off jerks.

"I think it's more that I swore off assholes."

"All men are assholes," Savannah stated evenly, the thick, impenetrable wall around her heart after being cheated on firmly in place. She didn't forgive or forget, and she'd never moved on from the prick who made her hide her broken heart away from the world. Harper hoped that one day a good man would come along and help her sister heal. But, in the meantime, she was much more anti-men than Harper. Savvy thought they were all Satan's spawn.

Harper, on the other hand, was ready to dance with the devil. Especially since from the little she knew about Ryland, he couldn't be further from the 5'7" pretty boy who had used more facial products than she did.

And then there was the incredible swarm of butterflies that took flight every time she saw Ryland. Indescribable yumminess.

30

"Just be careful," Savannah said. "No good ever comes from opening your heart to the wrong person."

"I know. But we have to be hopeful, right?"

Savannah just snorted and shook her head.

"Look at Mom and Dad," Harper reminded her. "They had a great relationship and loved each other so much."

"They were one in a million," Savannah said softly.

Charlie and Libby Grant were the exception to the rule. They were high school sweethearts, married right after graduation and assumed they'd immediately start a family. But after years of trying, Libby never conceived and they eventually gave up. Then, at forty-four, she suddenly and miraculously got pregnant with Savannah, and Harper followed less than two years later.

When their mom passed away a little over a year ago, their dad followed three months later. It's like he couldn't live without her. They were the perfect example of true love. Harper wished they could've had more time with them. More time to make more memories. The ones she had were wonderful but didn't seem nearly enough to soften the blow of losing them both.

They needed new memories now, and it's why Savannah named the restaurant Charlie's Place, after their dad. Everyone was always welcome in their home and often neighbors would come over and hang out, affectionately telling their friends they'd see them at Charlie's place. Opening the restaurant in honor of their parents was something both girls really wanted, and now Savannah was running into all sorts of difficulties.

"I'm going to help you get this place up and running," Harper assured her sister. "Whatever it takes, we'll get it done. For Mom and Dad."

"Thanks, sis." Savannah slung an arm around Harper's shoulders and the sisters leaned their heads together. "Sorry, I'm so anti-men lately. I hope you have fun on your date tomorrow."

An image of Ryland's cobalt blue eyes filled Harper's head and she grinned. "I have a feeling it could be the start of something good."

"I hope so."

"Maybe he has a cute friend." Harper nudged her sister.

"Not interested."

"Hmm, that's what you say now, but if he has some hot former SEAL buddy, you might change your tune."

"Don't hold your breath." Savannah slid a fresh piece of sandpaper over to Harper. "Get working. We have a lot to do."

"Aye-aye, sis." Harper gave her a sloppy salute and then began to sand the hell out of the bartop, her thoughts inevitably drifting back to Ryland and their upcoming date. She had high hopes and it was time for her luck to change.

And, hey, I could use a little excitement in my life.

Chapter Three

At exactly 4 PM, Ryland and his team sat down at the rectangular table and waited while Banshee, their impressive tech guru, set up the call with their handler. Ryland knew Banshee had to be former intelligence of some kind. With that laptop of his, the man could find a needle in a haystack while blindfolded and his hands tied behind his back while whistling "Zip-a-dee-doo-dah." Quite simply, Banshee was the best and he could find or hack anything. He was also the voice in their ear on missions and Ryland appreciated his calm, steady approach to every job they undertook.

They all went by code names, and unlike military nicknames, they were able to choose these. So instead of some dumbass embarrassing callsign dropped on them because they fucked something up, they picked ones they actually wanted.

Ryland, AKA Rip, looked over the group gathered and felt just as comfortable in their combined capabilities and skill set as he had with his former SEAL team. They were developing that special bond that eventually happens to tight teams over time, and the teasing and banter was becoming second nature as they got to know each other better. The comfort started making him wonder what their real names were, where they lived, what they liked to do in their spare time. And those were dangerous thoughts when their orders were to avoid personal relationships.

Ex Nihilo, the name of their team, meant "Out of Nothing" in Latin. Personal lives stayed off the table. For the most part, anyway. Tanner and Ryland were the clear exception and they tried not to broadcast it too much, but he had a feeling the others knew.

Don't ask, don't tell. It was their motto.

The name Ex Nihilo sounded cool as shit. Too bad nobody could ever remember it. They were always debating on the right way to pronounce it and every time Pharaoh educated them, somebody forgot. Finally, Tanner started calling them the Ex Men because it was easier. And, of course, that pissed off Bruja, the lone female member of their team.

Bruja was a feisty Latina beauty with long, silky ebony hair that was always swept back in a ponytail and big, brown eyes. But Ryland knew better than to let her good looks deceive him. She was a martial arts expert trained in Krav Maga and could outclimb all of them on the rock wall. She may be the only woman on the team, but that didn't make her any less competent or lethal than the men. In fact, Ryland thought she might be the scariest of them all. Her codename meant "Witch" in Spanish and she could kick or bewitch the shit out of anyone. It was all a part of her murderous charm.

If Ryland had to guess, the smooth, confident man called Pharaoh had to be a former commander of some kind. The perfect team leader, he was always the epitome of calm and cool under pressure. Hella smart, too. But one look from his intense gray gaze could bury anyone. Pharaoh possessed an air about him that clearly communicated he was used to giving orders. He held himself like a leader, always spewed words of wisdom, and whenever he opened his mouth, everyone leaned forward a little and listened more closely. The man demanded respect and Ryland had never seen anything ruffle him in the six months they'd worked together.

Across from Pharaoh sat Saint, a broody SOB with coal black hair, fathomless dark eyes and endless ink over his hands and forearms. He spoke with a faint, undefinable accent and reeked of danger and cigarette smoke. He never got too friendly or joked around too much and had a sarcastic streak that could skewer someone. Ryland was glad Saint was on their side. The dude was ruthless.

The final member of their squad was Tanner "Mayhem" Stiles. Ryland's BFF resembled some sort of Norse Viking with his blond locks that hung in his ice blue eyes. Laidback and easygoing like Ryland, he gave off the impression that he didn't have a care in the world. But put a weapon in his hands and he was quick to show just how capable he was and exactly why The Agency had recruited him. When he wasn't surfing or joking around, Tanner was deadly. They all were.

Together, the six of them were the deadliest group of assassins ever put together by the U.S. government. Their job was to eliminate enemies of the United States by sneaking in and out and neutralizing their targets before anyone was the wiser.

And the best part was they didn't have to play by the rules of engagement.

The team flew all over the world and did things that other people couldn't in order to preserve freedom and justice. It wasn't a job for the meek or weak of stomach. Last week, Ryland slit a man's throat from ear to ear without thinking twice. But calling him a man humanized him when he was in fact a disgusting, piece of shit human trafficker with a mansion full of chained-up, underage girls.

Ex Nihilo swept in under the cover of night and took out the trash. They skimmed the pond of scum and didn't lose a wink of sleep afterwards.

They weren't just shadows who came to take down the worst of the worst. They were the darkness itself and would slither in through the keyhole and end the bad guys before they even knew what the hell was happening.

So far, Ex Nihilo had successfully executed twelve missions and The Agency considered them a massive success.

As Banshee finished hooking up wires and doing tech stuff that Ryland didn't understand, he glanced over at Bruja who was playing around with her nunchucks. She wielded them with unparalleled skill and Ryland was quite happy to be on the friendly side of her and her weapon.

When her dark gaze met his, she grinned. "You talk to Barbie yet, Rip?" she asked teasingly. "Or are you still too scared?"

"Yeah, what's up with that? You wait much longer and maybe you could take her to a four o'clock dinner over at Denny's on senior discount Tuesday," Banshee added and everyone laughed.

So much for keeping their personal lives quiet. Tanner had outed Ryland last week when he started teasing him about not having asked Harper out yet.

"Go ahead, laugh it up, but first, are you two dating anyone?" Neither said anything and Ryland gave them a smug look. "That's what I thought. And, for your information, I talked to Harper today, thank you very much, and we have a date tomorrow night."

"My man!" Tanner exclaimed and slapped hands with Ryland.

Across the table, Saint merely rolled his eyes and Pharaoh smirked.

"Poor girl has no idea what she's getting into," Bruja stated, spinning her nunchucks.

"Oh, she knows," Ryland assured her.

"Barbie's about to get the whole package," Tanner said, backing up his friend.

"That's right." Ryland and Tanner exchanged a complicated maneuver of slides, bumps, and snaps ending with splayed fingers and a mutual shout of "Pow!" at the end.

"Is this meeting going to start any time this century?" Saint cracked his neck and looked more bored than a kid forced to sit through church.

"Hey, Saint," Ryland said, "if you ever need any help removing that pole from your ass, Mayhem and I could help."

Saint lifted his inked middle finger in response just as the incoming call buzzed. Pharaoh reached over and flipped a switch, connecting the team with their mysterious handler, known to them only as Merlin.

"Sir, you're on speaker," Pharaoh said, instantly all-business. "The team's all here, ready to go."

"Good then let's not waste any time," the distorted voice said, its true tone hidden by a mechanical filter. None of them had ever met or seen Merlin. He was the man behind the curtain who gave them their orders. Pharaoh was the only one who had a contact number for the man, but his true identity was a mystery. The team figured he'd been recruited just like them and was most likely former military. Although, they weren't exactly sure why the cloak and dagger routine was necessary.

"You're going to fly to Abu Dhabi and eliminate Yusuf Bashar, an arms dealer selling weapons to Syrian terrorists. I'll be supplying you with the codes and any other intel needed to break into his heavily-guarded compound. Once you eliminate Bashar, you come back home. Couldn't be any more clear cut. Any questions?"

Pharaoh looked down the table at his teammates and was greeted by the expected silence.

Cake walk. They'd be in and out with no one the wiser. They were like wraiths, capable of carrying out straightforward missions like these in their sleep.

"Roger that," Pharaoh said. "When do we leave?"

"ASAP."

Ryland's jaw dropped. *What the fuck?* He had a date to go on tomorrow night with Harper and now he was going to be stuck in goddamn Abu Dhabi. By the time they flew there, completed the op and returned home, he wouldn't be able to take her out until at least Saturday night.

"Acknowledged."

"The plane will take off as soon as you arrive at the airport."

Fucking great. Ryland glared down at the tabletop. They shouldn't have left until next week. They'd been averaging two missions a month and this was pushing things into frequent flier mile territory.

The moment Pharaoh disconnected the call, Ryland let out a low groan.

"Looks like your date just got canceled, Rip. Too bad." Saint sent him a smirk.

"I thought we were leaving next week." Ryland didn't want to sound like a whiny bitch, but he didn't appreciate the lack of notice. Despite what The Agency thought, they did have lives.

"Maybe they're nervous Bashar will disappear," Banshee offered, pushing his dark-rimmed glasses up his nose.

Ryland gave a derisive snort.

41

"Sorry, Rip," Bruja commented. "But the world's baddies don't take your dating life into consideration."

"Things change and we adapt. We all know that," Pharaoh stated. "I suggest we get moving."

With a low growl, Ryland stood up. There was nothing he could do except go with his team. He couldn't return home first and ask Harper if they could push their date back, and he didn't have her number to call and cancel.

He felt bad, but he'd explain that work took him on a last-minute trip out of the country. He'd make it up to her later. In the meantime, Bruja was right. There were bad guys out there who needed to be stopped and his job was to hunt them down and eliminate them. It was time to suck it up and focus on the mission ahead.

Maybe if he was lucky, he'd be the one to take the kill shot. A little extra vengeance on this fucker Bashar who just screwed up his entire weekend.

But it was like Pharaoh said. Adapt and move forward.

The team said goodbye to Banshee, who would direct them from their home base, and then split up into two SUVs provided by The Agency which took them to the private airport where they would fly out. Just like they'd been doing for the past six months. No doubt, their pilot would be the same guy as every other mission The

Agency sent them on. No one knew anything about him except that his code name was Phantom. He never got personal, but the confidence he oozed led Ryland to believe he was former military and he was extremely skilled at his job.

Sitting in the backseat and staring out the SUV's dark-tinted glass, Ryland mentally prepared himself for the mission ahead. They were all quiet, focused, ready to do what needed to be done. After a stop at the storage unit to gear up, they'd get on the plane and settle in for the long trip. Once they arrived at the private airstrip in Abu Dhabi, they'd head straight to Bashar's compound.

Then it was time to take out the trash.

Chapter Four

The long flight to the Middle East was a pain in the ass, but Ryland was used to it. They all were and no one minded it too much. It was just something they'd all come to expect. A part of the job. The one thing he couldn't get used to was the climate. It was June which put the Persian Gulf city squarely on the same latitude as the devil's doorstep. They might have the same sunny blue skies as San Diego, but the extreme heat and humidity made Ryland's hair start to wave the second he stepped off the plane.

Already sweating, he swiped a hand across his forehead and glanced up at the unforgiving sun. The capital city of the United Arab Emirates might be luxurious, but they could have it. It was just after noon and the unbearable heat beat down with relentless force. It was the kind of oppressive heat that made you sweat in places you didn't even know you could sweat, and ratcheted up your core temp until your blood felt like it was boiling.

Climbing into their two waiting SUVs, the complaints immediately started.

"Fucking hot armpit of a country," Ryland growled.

"Hey, look at the bright side. At least we're not crawling around on some goddamn mountain or searching caves," Tanner commented.

Ryland looked over at his friend who'd barely broken a sweat. As usual, he looked like a half-frozen Norse Viking with his frosty blue eyes. "How is it that my balls are sweating and you look cool as a cucumber?"

Tanner chuckled. "The heat agrees with me."

"You can fucking have it," Saint grumbled, grumpy as always, sweat rolling down his temples. He hadn't had a cigarette in hours and that only contributed to his foul mood.

At least Ryland wasn't the only one feeling like a half-cooked turkey. He wished he were up to his chin in an ice bath.

"At least you don't have to deal with boob sweat," Bruja grumbled as she adjusted her bra.

Ryland shook his head and chuckled. "True. But I

think ball sweat is pretty close. Just on a smaller scale."

"A much smaller scale," Bruja commented with a grin.

Pharaoh drove them straight to the safe house where they would go over the mission and wait until dark. At that time, they would drive to Yusuf Bashar's compound, infiltrate it and neutralize the arms dealer.

At least, that's what should have happened.

The minute they walked into the stifling-hot safe house, Pharaoh received an incoming call from Merlin. Ryland flipped the air conditioning on and the team waited while their leader conversed with their handler. If the out of the ordinary communication wasn't enough of a harbinger of the chaos to come, the dark look that came over Pharaoh's face certainly was.

After hanging up, their leader turned to his team and said, "Change of plans."

They all exchanged uneasy glances. A minor change, they could deal with. They'd all had to pivot during a mission at one time or another, but if it was anything major, that wasn't good news. Too much planning went into these missions, and precision was a key factor of their success. He gritted his teeth and listened as Pharaoh shared the new details.

"Bashar isn't at his compound. He's at his

apartment in the city." Everyone waited for him to continue. "Seven floors from the top of Etihad Towers."

"Fuck me," Saint hissed. "And we're just supposed to waltz right in and shoot this bastard between the eyes? How?"

"Let's call Banshee and come up with a new plan." Pharaoh glanced down at his large G-Shock. "And we better have one in five hours."

"What's in five hours? Hell, it won't even be dark by then," Ryland said.

"That's when Bashar is scheduled to leave and catch a flight to South America."

Fucking hell. Ryland pinched his brow and exchanged a look with Tanner. Saint kicked a nearby chair which Bruja deftly snagged, spinning it around and sitting down at the table, while Pharoah opened his laptop and dropped into a chair beside her.

"Banshee," Pharaoh said after the video call connected, "we need all the intel you can pull up on Etihad Towers. That's our new target site to neutralize Bashar."

"Etihad Towers?" Banshee echoed. "On it."

Ryland, Tanner and Saint joined Pharaoh and Bruja in seats around the table, waiting while Banshee collected the information. They would get their hands on the building's schematics easily enough, but Ryland hoped Banshee would have enough time to hack into Bashar's system and get them the passwords and codes necessary to unlock doors. Otherwise, this op could go FUBAR fast. And Ryland was starting to have a bad feeling twist his gut.

"There are three residential towers," Banshee said, fingers flying across a couple different keyboards. "Our man Bashar's apartment—and I use the term lightly—is located on floors 129-133. FYI, it's over 29, 000 square feet of pure luxury and Abu Dhabi elegance and perched 1500 feet above the city."

"Christ," Pharaoh mumbled and swiped a hand through his dark hair.

Ryland didn't like seeing their team leader ruffled. The dude never looked bothered by anything, so when he was, Ryland took note, concern edging in fast.

"That's a lot of square footage to cover," Bruja stated, a frown marring her forehead. "How many floors total again?"

"One-hundred forty," Banshee replied.

"There are only five of us here," Tanner said. "What the hell? That place is probably swarming with security. In the lobby alone!"

"So, we avoid the lobby," Saint said easily, leaning

back and lacing his fingers behind his head. "I might be able to get us in another way."

"Explain," Pharaoh demanded.

"Through a window."

"A window?" Ryland repeated blankly. "On the 129th floor? We gonna sprout wings and fly up there?"

"What's your plan?" Pharaoh crossed his muscled arms, exposing his dagger tattoo.

"We become window cleaners for the day."

For a moment, no one said anything.

"I think I'd rather go in guns blazing," Tanner said.

Ryland knew his friend was quick to jump into the action, but this op was going to require some extra finesse since they were potentially going up against a lot of tangoes at once. Plus, he had the inside knowledge that Tanner wasn't a big fan of heights.

"Saint might be onto something," Pharaoh said, mulling the idea over.

"I'll do it," Ryland offered. "Heights don't bother me."

"I don't mind them either." Bruja drummed her fingers on the tabletop. "We don't have a lot of options and time is ticking, fellas."

"It's a good idea," Banshee said. "If you guys can get up to Bashar's floor and get inside from the outside, I'll make sure the alarm and cameras are disabled."

"Piece of cake," Saint said arrogantly. "Who's ready to hang off the side of a building?"

"Rip and Saint, you two go in as window washers," Pharaoh stated. "Bruja and I will have eyes on security. Mayhem, keep the getaway car running and ready to roll."

"Roger that."

******

Standing outside of Etihad Towers, that gnawing feeling in Ryland's gut returned. He pushed it aside, ignoring it to focus on the semi-plan they had in place, assuring himself this was merely business as usual. Sure, plans were changed at the last minute, but the new plan was a good one.

At least, that's what he kept telling himself.

Situated in Abu Dhabi's exclusive district of Ras Al Akhdar, Etihad Towers was comprised of five total buildings: three for residential living, one hotel and one business center. They were surrounded by impeccably landscaped gardens and located near the beach and largest shopping mall in the city. They screamed decadence and excess, and they were a practical hive of activity.

After the team split up, Ryland and Saint followed Banshee's instructions, weaving through tourists and locals, and confidently making their way around the building to a back door used by employees only. In that short amount of time, Saint managed to inhale almost an entire cigarette. *Disgusting.*

"Those things'll kill you, you know. It's called lung cancer."

Saint chuckled and flicked the remainder of the still burning cigarette into a potted plant. "Seriously? You really think I have a better chance of dying that way than getting a bullet to the head?"

Ryland rolled his eyes and pushed through the large door. The window washers' normal working day was over, but who would really stop and ask questions when they were hanging outside the building?

They each slipped into a pair of workman's overalls, grabbed buckets and squeegees, and carried their backpacks over to the freight elevator which was used by workers and deliverymen. As expected, they were completely ignored. Just two more worker bees blending into the background. The building was 140 floors total and by the time they reached the roof, Ryland was mentally running through the schematics and technical specs of Bashar's apartment seven floors below.

They walked over to the building's edge and Ryland scratched his head. "Where's the platform?"

"That's not how they roll here." Saint shoved a harness at Ryland.

Ryland's mouth edged up in a daredevil grin. "Hell yeah."

"I thought you might like this, you adrenaline junkie."

"Sign...me...up." Ryland stepped into the harness, secured it, then checked his ropes, knots and carabiners, giving Saint a thumbs-up once everything was in place.

"Rip and Saint are in position on the roof," Saint reported.

"Roger," Pharaoh answered. "Bruja and I have eyes on security."

"Cameras are looping and I'm in their feed," Banshee informed them.

"Rip and Saint, you guys are a go," Pharaoh said.

Swinging his long legs over the ledge, Ryland turned, planted his boots on the building and leaned back. When he looked down, his stomach did a small flip. *Talk about fucking high.* He could see the curvature of the Earth.

And he loved it.

He supposed he was a bit of an adrenaline junkie. He'd done everything from skydiving to bungee jumping to swimming with sharks. Scaling an impossibly high structure was just one more notch on his extreme experiences bedpost. Not much scared or fazed him.

People like Yusuf Bashar, though…

They were the ones who put cold fear in Ryland's heart. Their evil ways brought true terror into the world. And that's why he vowed to take them down.

As they began to descend, Ryland realized it was a lot like rappelling. Counting the floors as they lowered, he pictured where they'd be breaking in—the music room window on the 133rd floor. They figured it would most likely be empty since Bashar didn't play any instruments.

At least they hoped.

"How long do you think it takes them to clean all these windows?" Ryland mused.

Banshee was in his ear with an answer practically before Ryland finished his question. "It takes two and a half months to clean all 20,000 windows and when they're finished, they start all over again."

"Huh. Aren't you just full of useless knowledge?"

"That's my job."

"Banshee, are we clear?" Saint asked calmly.

"I've got eyes everywhere and closest tango is on the 132nd floor. One-three-three is clear. Be careful, boys."

"Roger."

Ryland and Saint stopped their descent and swayed outside the window. The wind had begun to pick up but Ryland ignored it, focusing completely on the mission. Pulling his backpack around, he removed a small drill and used it to remove the bolts holding the window in place. Then he and Saint replaced the existing bolts with custom bolts buffered with rollers. Carefully, they pried at the window corners and popped the pane free. Using the rollers, they pulled it forward, leaving just enough room for them to slip inside.

With his feet back on the ground, Ryland unbuckled his harness and shrugged it off. He pulled his backpack back on and removed the Glock 19, equipped with a silencer, from its holster.

Time to go hunting.

Ryland and Saint moved forward through the enormous music room, skirting a Grand piano, a harp and velvet upholstered chairs. A crystal chandelier dominated the ceiling and an enormous tapestry, no doubt priceless, hung on one of the gilded walls. Not a speck of dust on any surface.

The place was way too rich for his blood.

In his head, Ryland once again pictured the layout of the 133rd floor: music room, grand salon library, media room with theater that seated 100 people, observatory, private reception gallery and guest and staff bedrooms.

He and Saint walked into the hallway on silent feet, communicating with hand signals. Saint might be an arrogant, moody asshole at times, but the man was a fearless and skilled pro, and Ryland respected the hell out of him.

Ignoring the elevator, they found the back staircase reserved for the staff and headed down.

"You've got a tango approaching from the east," Banshee informed them. "Watch your six."

Ryland had full confidence that Saint had his back and vice versa. Though the team had only been working together for six months, they were the best of the best. And for missions like these, confidence in your fellow team was crucial.

Moving forward, Ryland took point and Saint covered their asses. The 132nd floor was mostly bedrooms, multiple dressing rooms and a gaming room. The moment they spotted the tango, Ryland fired and took him down with two shots—one to the head, one to the chest. He dropped hard and fast and they skirted around him, heading straight for Bashar's bedroom.

"How many in the master suite?" Ryland asked.

"Two," Banshee reported.

"Roger."

So far, so good. If Bashar was in the bedroom, they could wrap this up fast. If not, they would move down another level and methodically clear the study, private gym, catering kitchen, massive ballroom and outdoor terrace until they found their target.

Clearly, being an arms dealer and selling weapons to terrorists paid well. It made Ryland sick to his stomach. He knew good men who had died because the bad guys had weapons they shouldn't have had access to. All thanks to fuckers like Yusuf Bashar.

And really? Who needs to live like this? he thought derisively, eyeing an ugly statue on a pedestal with a light shining down on it. A part of him wanted to smash it just for fun. Instead, he kept moving and paused directly outside the open door to Bashar's bedroom.

After communicating with a look, Ryland and Saint swept into the room. A big security guard was standing near the door and the moment he saw them, he reached for his weapon. But he wasn't fast enough. Ryland took him out with two swift shots while Saint moved past the falling body and right into the bedroom.

Two more muffled shots filled the air.

Ryland touched his ear comms. "Two more tangoes down."

"Do you have eyes on Bashar yet?" Pharaoh asked.

Ryland followed Saint, pausing in the doorway. He'd taken down another tango, but it wasn't Bashar.

"Negative."

Together, they headed out and toward the back staircase, down to the next level.

Come out, come out wherever you are, you piece of shit. Ryland moved down the steps fast and smooth, back to the wall, pistol ready, Saint following. Until now, Ryland had tried to ignore the strange feeling in his gut when the mission parameters suddenly changed. But, dammit, that little niggling always seemed to know.

And now that small itch that something wasn't right turned into a full-blown, massive blaze of epic proportions as Banshee's voice crackled through their earpieces, "Fuck! Twenty more tangoes just popped up out of nowhere! You guys need to get the fuck out of—"

Silence.

Ryland abruptly stopped and exchanged a surprised look with Saint. He pressed his comms, "Banshee?"

No answer.

Pharaoh's voice cut through. "Abort! Rip and

Saint—abort!"

Chapter Five

"Fuck!" Ryland hissed.

"Lung cancer, huh?" Saint spun and they raced back up the stairs.

But slipping back out the way they came in suddenly wasn't an option anymore. Five tangoes appeared on the staircase above them. Gunfire erupted and two bullets hit Ryland in the chest. The impact of the slugs knocked him backwards and his knees buckled.

Christ. The pain was like a lightning bolt to his sternum and he couldn't catch a breath. Thank God the bullets only hit his tactical vest. But they still held a bitch of a punch.

Saint charged straight up the steps, shooting like a suicidal madman. Kneeling, Ryland lifted his Glock and fired on the tangoes.

"We're coming up!" Pharaoh shouted in their comms.

"Hurry the fuck up!" Ryland yelled, grabbing the railing and pulling himself up. He raced after Saint, both of them continuing to fire their weapons, forcing the two remaining tangoes to flee for cover. But the moment they hit the next floor, a new swarm of guards appeared on the landing below.

Shit. Not good.

They were outnumbered and nearly surrounded. With no other choice, they kept running up and darted back into the music room. That's when Ryland noticed the blood seeping through Saint's sleeve.

"Get harnessed up. I'll cover you," Ryland said. Saint looked about to argue, but the blood gushing from his upper arm shut his mouth quick enough, and he did as Ryland said. Meanwhile, Ryland began firing into the hallway, trying to hold the inevitable assault off as long as possible, praying for their back-up to arrive but knowing it was beyond unlikely.

"I'm good!" Saint called. "C'mon!"

The tangoes continued their approach, being way too fucking bold, and Ryland knew he wouldn't have enough time to get fully and securely harnessed before he had to jump out the window. Glancing over his shoulder, he saw Saint now hanging outside, gun inside the window and ready to provide cover. God, he loved that moody, chain-smoking SOB. Running across the room, darting around the piano, Ryland yanked the harness off the floor and slipped out the window.

Saint started firing as Ryland jumped, holding onto the rope for dear life, and swinging out into thin air. *Just don't let me fall out.* He came flying back and slammed into the wall with an *oomph.* Using the pulley system, grateful for his upper arm strength, he jerked at the rope, tugging his big body up fast.

"We're pinned down," Bruja hissed into the comms.

"Where are you?" Ryland asked, arms burning, almost to the rooftop. He glanced down to find Saint right behind him. Ryland fired off a couple of shots to cover him.

"In the freight elevator. They locked it down."

"I'm going to see if I can unlock it," Tanner said. "Heading to the main security office on the ground level."

"Roger that, Mayhem. We're stuck on the 60th floor. And Pharaoh is wounded."

"How bad?" Ryland gritted out.

"Bullet graze," Bruja reported.

"Join the fucking club," Saint said dryly.

"I'm fine," Pharaoh said, but Ryland heard the strain in his voice. "Bruja is the one who got stabbed."

"Christ," Tanner swore.

"We're going to open the maintenance hatch and climb out of this tin can," Pharaoh informed them.

"What the hell happened?" Tanner asked no one in particular.

The silence that greeted his question spoke volumes. Ryland knew they were all thinking the same thing. All had the same sinking feeling they'd been set up. It's almost like Bashar's men had known they were coming.

Pulling himself over the edge, Ryland dropped onto the roof and let the harness fall. He turned, offered his hand to Saint and hauled him over.

"How's your arm?" Blood stained the upper sleeve of his jumpsuit.

"Fine," he growled.

Things were far from fine, though, especially when Tanner came through his comms. "Rip, Saint, armed guards are heading up the staircases and elevators are all on lockdown. You guys need to get out of there pronto."

The men exchanged a look. How the hell were they

62

supposed to escape?

"Elevator shaft?" Saint asked and Ryland gave a sharp nod.

They didn't have any choice and down was their only option. As they ran back outside to grab the window washer ropes and harnesses, Tanner's voice crackled in Ryland's ear. "I'm in the security office. It looks like I need a code to unlock the freight elevator."

Which wouldn't be a problem if they still had Banshee on the line.

"Roger," Ryland responded. "We're going to use the window washer ropes and go down the elevator shaft."

"Copy," Pharaoh responded. "See you at the rendezvous point."

They quickly gathered up the heavy ropes, tossed them over their shoulders and carried the huge coils back to the elevator. With a grunt, Ryland dropped his rope on the floor and reached for the elevator door.

"Help me pry it open!" Both he and Saint stuck their long fingers into the narrow jam and began to pull, forcing the steel door open. Ryland leaned forward and squinted, trying to see down into the dimly lit shaft where the elevator cab sat motionless eighty floors below them.

"This op just keeps getting better and better."

Ryland and Saint tossed their ropes down into the darkness then edged over the side and began to descend down into the shaft. From that height, it looked bottomless.

"That thing better not fucking start up again," Saint growled through gritted teeth, eyes on the cab below them.

"Don't even say it." Ryland lowered himself swiftly, using his fast-roping skills training. He'd done the same thing a million times and knew the proper technique. However, he was usually rappelling out of a helo and not down an elevator shaft.

"Cameras are back up," Tanner hissed in their ear. "I've got eyes on Bashar."

"Abort, Mayhem," Pharaoh growled.

"He's in the garage. I'm heading down."

"Mayhem!" Pharaoh snapped. "Goddammit! I said abort!"

Shit. Ryland knew Tanner was going to try to bring Bashar down on his own. And he hoped like hell his friend got the bastard. Pharaoh wouldn't be happy Tanner ignored his direct command, but if Tanner saw an opportunity, he would take it and get the job done. Mission fucking accomplished.

"Everyone to the rendezvous point *now*," Pharaoh

ordered.

Ryland and Saint were moving dangerously fast and when they reached the sixty-first floor, the door was still open where Pharaoh and Bruja had escaped. The men swung out of the shaft and their boots landed safely on the floor.

"That was fun," Saint commented dryly.

"Staircase?"

Saint pointed left and they jogged over, shoved through the door and into the stairwell. Moving fast, they pounded down, flight after endless flight.

"Goddammit. Could this building be any taller?"

Ryland heard Saint huffing beside him and smirked. "Out of breath from too many cigarettes, Saint?"

In answer, Saint increased his speed and flew forward, passing Ryland. It turned into a race down to the bottom level and, by the time they reached the garage, Ryland had surpassed him.

"C'mon, old man." Ryland waited in front of the exit door for Saint to reach his side and received a glare.

"Let's hope there's not a whole army down here waiting for us," Saint said, voice grim.

"No shit." Because that would really, really suck ass. He touched his comms and tried to contact Tanner but received no answer. Assuming his friend's comms didn't work down on the subterranean level, Ryland slowly pushed the door open.

They moved out fast and low, scanning the area for threats. It was eerily quiet and, a moment later, they ran into Pharaoh and Bruja.

"Where's Mayhem?" Pharaoh asked.

"Not sure," Ryland responded. "He's not responding."

"Bruja, get the car," Pharaoh ordered. "We'll get Mayhem."

While she jogged away, Ryland, Saint and Pharaoh moved forward in a single file, searching the strangely quiet underground garage. Without warning, three men stepped out from behind a large SUV and began firing. Ryland and his teammates dove behind the nearest car for cover and immediately returned fire.

Three shooters suddenly turned into five and that number doubled before Ryland could reload his pistol. "What the fuck?" he yelled. The moment he took one guard down, another one appeared. "They keep coming."

"We need to get out of here!" Saint shouted. "They're closing us in."

"We have to find Mayhem!" Ryland yelled over the pop of gunfire.

"Pull back," Pharaoh ordered.

Cursing under his breath, Ryland followed the order. He knew if he didn't, he'd be surrounded in less than thirty seconds. They reversed and moved sideways, crouching down and using the cars for cover as they put distance between them and Bashar's men. Turning his head to check the next row, Ryland spotted Tanner thirty feet away. He was down on the ground between two cars, blood pooling around his body.

Ryland froze, his blood turning to ice. He grabbed Pharaoh's shoulder, squeezed and yelled, "Cover me!" Without waiting for an answer, Ryland took off, leaving the cover of the vehicles to sprint across the wide-open area, taking the most direct route to his friend and teammate.

Thanks to the cover provided by Pharaoh and Saint, he made it to the other side, dropping down to his knees. "Tanner!" He flipped his friend over and Tanner's light blue eyes cracked open. A quick scan revealed Tanner had been shot too many times to count. Armor piercing rounds had shredded his vest.

No, no, no. Heart in his throat, Ryland pressed two fingers against Tanner's throat, searching for a pulse. It was so damn weak, he could barely feel it.

The entire situation seemed unreal. *This wasn't what was supposed to happen. How the fuck did this op go so off the rails?*

"Stay with me, bro," Ryland pleaded. "We're gonna get you out of here."

But Tanner's eyes slid shut again and Ryland couldn't tell if his friend's chest was still rising and falling or—

The sound of squealing tires filled the air and an SUV pulled up in front of him, the rear door flying open and Pharaoh jumping out before the vehicle even stopped. He ran over, helped Ryland pick Tanner up and they rushed him to the rear of the SUV where Saint helped pull him inside. Once they were all in, Bruja slammed on the gas and the car jumped forward.

"What in the fucking fuck of all clusterfucks just happened?" Bruja cried from the driver's seat.

The moment Ryland undid Tanner's tactical vest, more blood erupted from his various wounds. "Shit! Apply pressure. We need to stop the bleeding!"

The three men tried to staunch the wounds but, despite their best efforts, Ryland watched his best friend bleed out before his eyes.

"Fuck," Ryland hissed. "Tanner, c'mon."

Pharaoh checked the pulse at Tanner's neck. "He's gone." A muscle jerked in his cheek and he turned his head, avoiding eye contact with Ryland.

Saint punched a fist into the seat and Ryland could

only shake his head.

It had to be a mistake. There's no way Tanner was dead.

"No…no…" Ryland refused to accept it. "Tanner, you fucker, wake up!" His voice cracked and a rage like he'd never known before filled him. He grabbed Tanner's shoulders and shook him.

"Rip—" Pharaoh laid a hand on his shoulder.

"Not Tanner," Ryland mewled. "He was the good one."

Pharaoh squeezed Ryland's shoulder as reality came crashing down all around him.

"We still have bad guys to take down…and waves to catch…" Ryland's fingers curled into Tanner's bullet-torn t-shirt and he bent over his best friend, feeling his warm blood soaking through the soft cotton.

Ryland let out a guttural roar and dropped his head between his shoulders.

Whoever did this would pay. And they would pay with blood.

******

They finally reconnected with Banshee on the flight home and exchanged every piece of information they had while Pharaoh kept trying to get ahold of Merlin.

But their handler wasn't answering.

That was their first clue that something had gone more than just sideways with the op. Merlin always answered.

"We were set up," Ryland said in a dull, lifeless voice. He sat on the floor beside the body bag that held Tanner while the others attended to their individual wounds. He'd never felt so numb in his life. Like someone had torn his heart out then anesthetized him.

Bruja knelt down beside him. "Come with me, Rip. Let's get you cleaned up."

Ryland glanced down and realized he was still covered in Tanner's blood. His stomach and heart revolted as one and he let Bruja help him up and guide him to the plane's bathroom. His emotions were cycling—first rage and anger followed by denial then grief and now a desolate sadness covered him like a burial shroud.

His best friend was gone.

"Wash up, okay?" She handed him a washcloth, gently squeezed his arm and then stepped out of the small area, pulling the door closed behind her. It was his first moment alone since finding Tanner in that godforsaken garage, and he stared at his reflection in the mirror.

Unshed tears brightened his cobalt eyes to a lighter,

brighter blue and he grit his jaw so hard he was surprised he didn't crack a tooth. *Why Tanner?* Ryland would rather it had been him.

Cursing under his breath, he pulled off the saturated coveralls followed by his blood-stained shirt and threw them in the trash. He never wanted to see any of it again. Moving in slow motion, he wet the washcloth and dragged it over his arms and chest, rinsing it until the water ran clear, then washed his hands again and again under the barely lukewarm water, scrubbing until his skin felt raw.

As the water turned colder, a burning need ignited inside of him. The need to find out who had done this to Tanner. Who had given them up to the wolves. Who was going to pay with their lives.

They'd been betrayed. Ryland knew it in his gut and, as a lone tear tracked down his stony face, he vowed revenge.

And payback would be a bitch. He'd make sure of that.

Chapter Six

Harper spent all Friday morning combing through her closet. She hated everything she owned. Deep down, she knew her wardrobe was fine, but that rational voice was drowned out by pre-date anxiety. Nothing was right for dinner with Ryland. When panic started screaming through her mind, she shut it up by convincing her sister to join her on a whirlwind shopping spree to find the perfect first date outfit.

Two hours later, Harper did a twirl in front of her mirror, finally satisfied with her choice. Savannah encouraged her to get something cute, not too sexy, but also not too prim either. After trying on a stack of clothes, Harper picked out a sundress that was flirty, fun and on sale. Paired with tall summer wedges she borrowed from Savannah, her legs looked a little bit longer and she loved that. She'd pulled her long blonde hair back in a high ponytail and kept her makeup light. She knew she'd spent way more time getting ready than she probably should have and her nerves were all over the place.

It was almost 6 PM and he'd be walking over soon. After a final quick check in the mirror, she brushed her teeth, grabbed her wristlet and sat down on the couch to wait.

And wait…and wait…

By 6:15, she convinced herself that he was running late.

By 6:30, she was pacing back and forth and looking out the window every ten seconds.

By 7:00, she kicked off her wedges and started worrying. What if something had happened to him? They hadn't exchanged numbers, so there was no way he could call and tell her something was wrong.

And by 9:00, she knew she'd been stood up. With a sigh, Harper peeled herself up off the couch, walked down to her bedroom and changed into her pajamas, feeling utterly dejected.

Unbelievable. Had he forgotten? Decided to cancel? Been called out of the country on a last-minute job to protect the country?

Yeah right. Wishful thinking.

The truth was she'd spent all day getting ready for their date and he hadn't even bothered to show up. What a jerk. He turned out to be everything she hoped he wouldn't be. The sad thing is she'd had such high hopes. There had been such a connection and chemistry between them. Was she the only one who'd felt something?

"Pathetic," Harper whispered to herself. Maybe this was a sign that she needed to forget about men and focus on herself. On *her* happiness.

With that thought firmly planted in her head, Harper stepped into her pink fluffy slippers and headed straight to the kitchen. Opening the freezer, she grabbed the pint of Ben & Jerry's Half Baked. The chocolate chip cookie dough/ fudge brownie mix was the ultimate comfort food to drown her sorrows.

But as she lifted her spoon, she paused right before taking a big bite. She didn't want a soothing sugar overload, she wanted answers. In fact, she deserved those answers. Shoving the tub of ice cream back into the freezer, she threw the spoon in the sink, pointed her pink slippers toward the door, and decided Ryland owed her an explanation.

When Patrick had tossed her out, she didn't question it or put up a fight. She'd merely hung her head, packed her bag and walked out. But, dammit, no more. She wasn't going to let another man get away with treating her like shit and making her feel bad about herself.

She deserved more; she deserved answers.

And screw it, she was going over to his apartment to get them.

******

Once they landed back in San Diego, the team headed straight to command central, the air between them heavy with sorrow. They'd lost one of their own and, though they'd all experienced it before, it never got any easier.

Especially when it was the guy you were buddies with.

Pharaoh looked up from the phone he'd been dialing nonstop for hours. Clearly, Merlin still wasn't answering. Which most likely meant he was dead or a part of the surprise strike against them.

And that twitchy feeling Ryland should have acknowledged hours ago was telling him their handler was a part of the ambush.

The team was upset about Tanner, frustrated over the entire op, and they needed answers. Banshee was working on it, using his hacking skills to run programs and dig up information about The Agency. But there was nothing the rest of them could do—at least not at the moment. And that didn't sit well with any of them.

Pharaoh moved up beside Ryland and laid a hand on his shoulder. "Go home and try to get some rest. We'll regroup in the morning. Figure out what the hell is going on."

Their gazes lowered to the body bag.

"I'll take care of Mayhem and—"

"His name was Tanner Stiles," Ryland interrupted heatedly. "He was more than some stupid nickname."

Pharaoh squeezed Ryland's shoulder. "Tanner will get the burial he deserves. And we'll all be there to show our respect."

Ryland gave a sharp nod. He knew Pharaoh was right. There was no way he'd be able to sleep, but at least he could take a hot shower and get the blood out from under his fingernails. It was starting to make him sick every time he looked down and saw it there.

He could channel his grief and frustration into thoughts of revenge.

By the time Ryland parked his Jeep and walked into his apartment, it was dark and he was exhausted. Instead of turning on the lights, he walked through the living room, memory and moonlight his only guides, planning to head straight to the bathroom.

At the last second, he turned, dropped his backpack and decided to grab a cold bottle of water from the fridge.

He spun around at a muffled *pop* and *whoosh*, clocking a dark shadow in his periphery, and dove sideways as another bullet flew past his head.

His fight mode and training kicking in, he stayed low, moving around the back of the couch, circling fast. He was glad he hadn't turned the lights on because the darkness provided cover. The intruder slunk forward, pistol raised in the direction Ryland had just vacated, and Ryland shot forward from the opposite side, slamming a fist against the asshole's wrist and forcing him to drop the gun.

Kicking it away, Ryland launched himself into the masked figure and they flew backwards, the intruder's back crashing into the coffee table and the glass shattering beneath him. They rolled sideways, fists flying, and Ryland managed to get several good hits in before the man punched him hard in the chin.

Ryland's head snapped to the side and stars danced at the edge of his vision, but it also gave him a clear line of sight to the gun. And it was within reach. Wasting no time, he grabbed it and spun. The fury inside him bubbled over to an all-consuming boil as he pulled the trigger.

The masked man dropped with a grunt of pain. Flipping on the light, Ryland was about to unmask the sonofabitch when he heard a knock at the door. *Shit.* The intruder was stunned, but still alive, and Ryland wanted to tie the bastard up and interrogate him.

But who the hell was at his door? As if in answer, the knock turned to a pounding and he heard a familiar, feminine voice.

"Ryland?"

Fuck. It was Harper.

"I know you're in there. I saw you walk in."

Talk about shitty timing.

"Uh, hang on," Ryland answered, reaching down and planning to drag the man out of Harper's sight.

"Are you avoiding me?"

"Oh, for fuck's sake," Ryland grumbled. Was she joking? He swiped a hand across his sweating brow and wondered if his day could get any worse.

The answer to that question was a resounding yes. The sneaky asshole at his feet was only pretending to be more hurt than he actually was. Spinning and doing some kind of martial arts move, the guy knocked Ryland right off his feet with a sweep of his leg.

More knocking. Damn, she was persistent.

With a grunt, Ryland rolled to the side, barely missing a swift kick to the gut. He still had the gun and he turned, fired off two more shots, and the intruder flew backwards and landed behind his couch.

Breathing hard, Ryland pulled himself to his feet, walked over and bent down to check the man's pulse. There wasn't one any longer. This time the fucker was dead. He yanked the mask up but didn't recognize the man. Who the hell was he? A nameless mercenary sent by whoever wanted his team dead?

Was The Agency behind all this? He raked a hand through his messy hair and knew they needed answers fast. But first he had to get rid of Harper.

Stalking across the living room, he yanked the door open, still panting, adrenaline from the attack pumping through him, and her aqua eyes widened.

"Uh, hi. I thought we had a date tonight," Harper said. He watched as the anger drained from her eyes and was replaced with something more closely resembling uncertainty. Or maybe concern.

Keeping the gun hidden behind the door, his gaze dipped. She was standing on his doorstep in a baby t-shirt, matching shorts and pink fuzzy slippers. Despite the dangerous situation, he couldn't help but notice how damn adorable she looked. Mouthwateringly adorable.

"Sorry, something came up." He knew it sounded lame, but he needed her to leave. *Now.*

A frown appeared between her brows. "Well, why didn't you just tell me?"

"Harper, can we talk about this later?"

"I don't think—" Her words abruptly cut off and she leaned closer, taking in his trashed apartment. "Is everything okay?"

Stepping sideways to block her view, he pulled the door closed further. "Yeah. Someone broke into my apartment, but it's fine now."

"Someone broke in? Oh, my God, I thought this was supposed to be a safe complex."

Christ. Ryland pinched the bridge of his nose. "Harper, sweetheart, I need to make some very important calls. Right now. Can we please talk tomorrow?"

"Sure," she said slowly. Then her attention dipped and her jaw dropped.

And Ryland knew she just saw something she shouldn't have.

Glancing over his shoulder, he noticed the intruder's boots sticking out from behind the couch. *Fucking great.*

Harper's eyes grew big as saucers and she started backing away from him. "Maybe I shouldn't have come over," she murmured, then tripped over her own feet as she turned to flee. As she went down, Ryland lurched forward and caught her in his arms.

At the same time, a shot pierced the air beside them.

"What was that?" Harper asked, looking around, more confused than startled. But Ryland knew exactly what it was, and he scooped her up, tossed her over his shoulder and ran like hell.

"Ryland!" she cried, small fists gripping onto the back of his shirt. "Put me down!"

"Sorry, sweetheart," he rumbled. "Can't do that."

"Oh, my God, stop! I'm going to scream!"

"Be my guest. But I think you should know that pop you just heard? That was a gunshot. There are some bad guys after me—and now they're after you, too."

"Me?" she squealed, bouncing up and down against his back. "I didn't do anything!"

Ignoring her, Ryland switched the gun to the hand wrapped around Harper's legs and dug his keys out of his pocket as he raced for his Jeep. After unlocking it, he tossed Harper across the console and into the passenger seat. Then he dropped down into the driver's seat and set the gun on his lap.

"You have a gun," she said, voice low and shaky.

"Actually, I have two. One's in the holster at my back. Well, technically, three if you also count the one in my duffel bag in the back."

81

He hit the gas and they peeled in a circle, smoke pouring from the tires. Harper grabbed her seatbelt, fastening it fast. She was studying him closely in a way she never had before as she whispered, *"Who are you?"*

Before he could answer, his phone rang and he answered it through the car speaker. With hindsight, it probably hadn't been his wisest decision.

"Yeah?"

"You and your team have been compromised," an electronic voice said. It reminded him of the altered voice Merlin used, but it was slightly different.

"No shit. Who the hell is this?" Ryland snapped.

"There's been an order issued for Ex Nihilo's immediate termination. If you don't go off grid, they're going to find you, hunt every one of you down, and you will all die."

"Who. Is. This?" Ryland growled.

"And now the girl's a target, too."

Click. Ryland slammed a fist against the steering wheel after the line went dead. He looked over at Harper who stared at him, slack-jawed.

"Let me out," she ordered.

"Sorry, can't do that, sweetheart."

"Please." Her voice shook and he felt bad, but he couldn't let her return home.

He had to assume she was "the girl" the voice indicated and was on their radar now, too. Dammit, he didn't want her sucked into this madness. But if she was already, her days were most likely numbered without his help and protection. Because they were dealing with a serious threat. *FPCON Delta.*

"Where are we going?"

Good question. He had no idea, so he hit Pharaoh's number. It rang and rang then dropped into voicemail. Pharaoh always answered his phone. Usually on the first ring. A cold dread spread through him as he tried again, but to no avail. Mouth dry, fingers trembling slightly, he called Saint.

"Rip, where are you?" Saint answered, sounding out of breath.

"Just neutralized an intruder and made a run for it with my neighbor. How about you?"

"Ditto. Someone broke into my place and tried to take me out."

"Shit!" Ryland hissed. "We need to meet up and figure out what the hell is going on. Command center?"

"No, somewhere they won't connect to us. Somewhere safe."

"It's the middle of the night, Saint. Where do you suggest?"

When he remained silent, Harper spoke up. "I know a place."

Ryland glanced over at her. "Where?" he gritted out.

Chapter Seven

Maybe it was stupid, but Harper gave Ryland directions to her sister's restaurant. He and his friends needed somewhere safe to go, and apparently so did she. She wasn't sure what the hell she just got tangled up in but, for some inexplicable reason, she trusted Ryland. When she looked at him, she saw a good guy and she believed that to her core. Plus, he didn't have to save her back at the apartment complex. He could've just left her there and ran. That had to count for something, right?

Ryland parked the Jeep behind Charlie's Place, and Harper led him to the back door and unlocked it with the key Savannah insisted she have. As soon as they stepped inside, she reached for the lights and he placed his hand over hers, stopping her.

"No, don't." He moved farther into the building and

his phone started buzzing.

Harper's hand fell away from the light switch and she wrapped her arms around herself. A chill ran through her body and she began to chew her lower lip.

"Pharaoh, where are you?" Ryland answered. After listening for a moment, he cursed under his breath. "Saint and I were attacked, too."

He briefly filled him in on the attack then rattled off the address for the restaurant.

After he hung up, Harper frowned. "Who are these guys?"

"My team."

"And you can trust them?"

He sent her a funny look. "Of course."

"You're all former military?"

"Yes. No. I don't know," he replied without elaborating and stalked across the floor. "Is there a back room or somewhere we can go without being seen through the window?"

The large picture window in front was mostly covered in kraft paper but, apparently, he wanted somewhere more private. "Yeah, there's a banquet room in the back corner."

"Great," he murmured. "We'll set up in there."

Set up? "Set up what?"

"A temporary base of operations."

Oh, Lord. Savannah was going to kill her. "How long do you plan on staying here?"

He arched a dark brow. "Why? You wanna kick me out already?"

She placed a hand on her hip. "This is my sister's place. If she finds a bunch of squatters in here, she's going to kick my ass first and ask questions later."

"We're not squatters and we'll be gone by dawn. She won't even know we were here. Is that okay?"

That seemed reasonable enough, so Harper nodded.

"Thank you," he murmured.

Ryland introduced her to his team as they arrived, starting with Saint who was followed closely by Banshee, Bruja and then Pharaoh. Figuring they were all callsigns of some type, she nodded at each of them as they gave her a cursory once-over before heading to the back room, setting up a table and chairs and hooking up their laptops.

Bruja, the woman with the striking caramel-colored eyes, focused her attention on Harper, taking in the pajamas. "You must be Barbie," she said before turning to Ryland. "Why is she here?"

Harper bristled with annoyance. The question had been directed to Ryland, but she narrowed her eyes and answered herself. "Because *Barbie* is the one who is letting you use this place as your base of operations. Temporarily. You'll have to be out by dawn."

Bruja's gaze met hers and Harper saw instant respect there. When she glanced over at Ryland, his lips were twitching.

"You heard her," Ryland said, backing her up. "We've got a few hours, so let's figure some shit out."

They took their places around the table and Ryland motioned for Harper to sit next to him, which made her feel...special. Maybe it was silly, but after standing up to the tough-looking woman with the dark hair, Harper was proud of herself. Just because she had blonde hair didn't mean she was some sort of airhead who didn't know what she was talking about or how to do anything worthwhile.

And Ryland looked pleased with her, too, which made Harper inwardly grin.

"Okay, let's go over what we know," Pharaoh said. He was at the head of the table beside Banshee who was tapping away on two different laptops. Pharaoh possessed an air of authority and Harper instantly pegged him as their leader. He oozed confidence and authority.

"What about her?" Saint asked, glancing over at Harper. She wasn't sure how she felt about the dangerously attractive man covered in tattoos. Everything about him was dark from his eyes to his hair to his clothes to his broody expression. Something about him screamed villain. Or anti-hero. She hadn't decided yet. But she was definitely a little scared of him.

"I won't tell anyone what you discuss," Harper said.

"That's not what I'm asking." Saint focused on Ryland. "You shouldn't have dragged her into this shit show."

"I didn't plan on it, but here we are. So she goes wherever we go," Ryland stated firmly then met Harper's surprised gaze. "Sorry, Harper, but whoever called me earlier said you're in trouble, too. If we leave you here without protection…well, I won't."

As much as she appreciated that, she couldn't just pick up and leave. Could she? She supposed if the alternative was a bullet in the head, she could. Besides, now wasn't the time to argue and be a pain in the ass, so she gave a slight nod and let the team carry on.

"Rip, tell us exactly what this caller said to you." Pharaoh assumed control of the discussion and the room once again. Harper studied him—from his thick, dark hair with a slight wave to his intense silver-gray eyes—and decided she liked him. Like Ryland, Pharaoh came across as a protector through and through, and that made her feel safe.

At least as much as possible considering there was now a target on her head.

"He used a voice changer app and said the team was compromised. That an order was issued for Ex Nihilo's immediate termination and if we didn't go off grid, they'd hunt us down and kill us."

"Let's assume The Agency ordered this. Any speculation on who the caller was? Who would tip us off and why?" Pharaoh asked, drumming his long fingers on the table top.

"Merlin?" Bruja offered.

"Could be anyone. We don't even know who makes up The Agency," Saint commented.

"Not yet," Banshee countered and cracked his knuckles above the keyboard. "I've got programs running right and left and, if all goes according to plan, I'll get past The Agency's firewalls and find some answers."

"Time frame?" Pharaoh asked.

Banshee shrugged and adjusted the glasses perched on his nose. "Depends. Their security is tight, but I'm better."

"Modest, too," Saint remarked dryly.

"I'm too damn good to waste time on modesty, Saint."

"Let's hope so," Saint said.

"Merlin never answered my calls so either he's cut ties with us or he's dead. Right now we can't afford to trust anyone except each other."

"So we think the entire Abu Dhabi op was a setup?" Ryland asked. "Because if it was, and if he is alive, we can't trust Merlin. He's the one who gave us bad intel."

"Exactly," Pharaoh stated.

Harper sat back, listening closely as the team discussed everything that had happened over the last twenty-four hours. When she discovered they'd lost one of their teammates, the situation took a very real and threatening turn in her mind. Plus, she couldn't forget the man lying on the floor in Ryland's living room. Whatever was happening was deadly serious.

She studied Ryland from the corner of her eye and, at the mention of Tanner's name, his composure slipped a notch. His jaw tightened and his shoulders tensed, but he masked his emotion quickly. She remembered him briefly mentioning the name before. Was Tanner the buddy he would surf with?

They were a resilient group, but they had to be hurting. And, if she had to guess, Ryland was hurting the most. She could feel it.

Since there was nothing they could do until Banshee

found something useful in his searches, Pharaoh advised them to try and get some shuteye. They'd regroup in an hour unless there was a breakthrough sooner. There was no way Harper could sleep, but she stood up and Ryland placed a hand on her back, guiding her into the main dining room area where it was dark.

Pharaoh and Banshee stayed in the backroom and kept working, while Bruja found a quiet corner and stretched out on the hard floor. Saint disappeared out a side door.

"Where's he going?" she asked.

"Out to smoke."

"Oh." Harper pointed toward the kitchen. "Are you thirsty? There's some bottled water in the kitchen."

"Sure, thanks."

He followed her to the other side of the unfinished restaurant and through the swinging kitchen door. Since it was hidden from the street, she flipped the switch and the overhead lights turned on. There were two bottles of water stashed in the large steel fridge and she handed one to Ryland.

"I'm sorry about all this, Harper."

"It's not your fault. Not entirely. I'm the one who came charging over like a bat out of hell." She hopped up on the counter and looked down at her slippered feet. "I thought you stood me up and…well, I was pissed."

"You would've had every right to be pissed." He cracked the water open and took a long drink.

Harper couldn't tear her eyes away from the movement of his throat as he pounded the water down. He drank nearly the entire thing in several long swallows and she gripped the edge of the counter tighter, her gaze moving up to where his lips circled the bottle.

She liked his lips. A lot. They weren't too thin or too full, and they looked soft and kissable. She wondered how they would feel against her own. Would he be a demanding kisser, taking charge? Or would he be gentle, taking his time to delicately explore her mouth before moving to other—

Mentally chastising herself for where her thoughts were heading, she refocused. Ryland had lost someone tonight and here she was having inappropriate thoughts.

"I'm sorry about your friend," she said softly.

The sadness he'd shut down earlier resurfaced, but this time he didn't bother hiding it. "Tanner was my best friend." His voice was so quiet she had to lean closer to hear him. "He bled out in my arms tonight."

"Jesus." The pain in his voice was evident and, without thinking, she reached out to him. Her anger over being stood-up and terror over being placed in harm's way by Ryland faded to the background. He'd tragically lost someone close to him while she'd been stewing over a missed date. None of that seemed to matter much anymore.

Ryland took her hands and stepped closer, gaze searching hers. His cobalt eyes swam with hurt and her heart ached for him. Pulling him into an embrace, she wrapped her arms around him and he pulled her close, burying his face in the curve of her neck. They held each other, giving and receiving comfort, and Harper knew she'd do anything to help him.

To stay with him.

******

Harper's warm embrace was like a soothing balm to his ravaged soul. He breathed her soft vanilla scent in deeply, letting it wash over him, comforting his unsettled soul. He'd never experienced this kind of solace before— not from his parents, his sister, his friends or any lover he'd ever taken.

There was something indescribable about the way she felt in his arms. Like they were complimentary puzzle pieces clicking together. She felt fucking *right*. And that scared the shit out of him.

But now was not the time for feelings like that.

Pulling back, caught in her aqua stare, Ryland felt

his heart slam hard against his rib cage. His hands slid down to grasp her hips and his focus dropped to her full, tempting lips.

Not the time, he reminded himself firmly.

But he wanted to kiss her. Desperately.

No. He'd just lost his best friend, almost died himself, and he'd dragged this amazing woman down with him. He hated feeling so out of control. Despite all the uncertainty, though, he knew one thing for sure—he wasn't going to let her out of his sight until they stopped whoever was behind this betrayal. And maybe not even after that if she'd let him.

"I'm going to keep you safe, Harper. I promise you," he whispered, his attention moving to the bridge of her freckled nose.

And he'd die to do it.

Without a second thought.

Chapter Eight

The date they should've been on earlier happened anyway, just under very different circumstances. Ryland and Harper sat down on the floor, cross-legged, and spent the next hour talking instead of sleeping. He pushed his sadness over losing Tanner down, burying it deep for the time being and refusing to let his emotions rule. He had to stay sharp, focused and detached moving forward. First, he would get vengeance, then he would allow himself proper time to mourn his friend.

Chatting with Harper was a good distraction from the anguish in his heart. She was beautiful, smart, quick-witted and wasn't afraid to tell him exactly what she thought. It was a nice change from what he was used to. Most of the beach bunnies he knew just told him what they thought he wanted to hear. It was like they didn't even have a head on their shoulders, and that got old fast.

He felt more than a mere attraction to Harper and enjoyed her company immensely.

"Sounds like you two are close," Ryland commented after Harper shared more about her sister.

"Savannah is more than my sister. She's my best friend." Harper tucked her legs beneath her. "Now that our parents are gone, she's all I have left."

Once again, he was surprised by how similar they were. He'd shared how his parents had both died and his only family left was his sister Addison, but he didn't get into any specifics. That would open a whole can of worms. For now, it was best to keep it simple.

Damn, he had a lot of secrets.

"Are you close to Addison?" Harper asked.

Was he close to his big sister? The answer to that was tricky. "Yes...and no," he answered, striving for honesty.

She tilted her head. "What's that mean?"

"Addie is four years older than me, so we're close in years. But I don't see her that often anymore. After our mom died..." His voice trailed off because he wasn't sure how much to share. Should he tell her what his sister really did? How they fought and could never see eye to eye because of how she chose to make her money? That Addie had followed in their mother's footsteps and was a

97

renowned thief currently on the FBI's Most Wanted List?

Nah, probably shouldn't mention that.

"After our mom died," he repeated, "our jobs took us to separate cities. I guess we just sort of lost touch."

"That's sad," Harper said, leaning forward. "You should reach out to her. I mean, after all this is, ah, over."

Ryland wondered if Harper had any idea how long the op to infiltrate The Agency could actually take? Hell, he didn't even know. Months maybe? A year? He didn't want to mention that quite yet for fear she'd flip the fuck out. Especially because she was staying with him until it was over whether she liked it or not.

One thing at a time, he reminded himself. Compartmentalize the sorrow over Tanner, feed the need for vengeance, keep Harper safe and bring down the bad guys. It was a tall order, but this is where he not only excelled, he thrived.

"What's your tattoo mean?" she asked, checking out his forearm.

Ryland turned his arm, letting her see it better. "I was part of DEVGRU's Red Squadron and we called ourselves 'the tribe'. Our insignia was the Native American, so my team and I got a tomahawk."

She lightly caressed a finger over the design and her touch sent shockwaves through his system. Their gazes locked and he wondered if she felt the same spark?

"It's…a little intimidating."

The tattoo or me? he wondered, leaning closer, eyes on her mouth.

Pharaoh poked his head through the swinging door and they both jerked away from each other. Like they'd been caught doing something they shouldn't have been doing.

"Banshee hacked into The Agency. He found some files."

Ryland stood up, offering Harper his hand. She took it and he pulled her up, but before they followed Pharaoh, Ryland squeezed her hand and said, "You need to know some things about me. And my team."

"Okaaay." She eyed him curiously.

He didn't want to purposely scare her off, but he didn't want to lead her on, making her believe he was some kind of hero or good guy. Because he wasn't. Far from it. His job was to kill people. Granted, they were bad people, but not everyone would be able to accept that.

"The organization we work for technically doesn't exist."

"The Agency."

"Yeah. Our job is to eliminate bad people, Harper. Enemies of the United States. We follow our handler's orders and don't ask questions."

She nodded.

"I don't want you thinking I'm some good guy. What I do…" He pulled in a deep breath and chose his next words carefully. "It can take its toll on certain people."

"So, what're you saying? It's taking its toll on you?"

"No. I'm saying the exact opposite. Don't ever mistake me for some kind of hero, Harper."

******

After they all reconvened at the table in the back room, Harper surreptitiously watched Ryland. He sat ramrod straight, intensity rolling off him in waves. That last comment he'd made had her wondering what kind of things he'd done in his past. And currently still did. She knew as a SEAL, he would've gone into many dangerous situations and he probably even had to kill people. But they were bad people.

Right?

That's what he'd said, anyway.

"Do we really want her in here?" Saint asked, his

onyx gaze fixed on Harper.

"She's involved," Ryland stated. "Whether we like it or not. So she may as well be in the loop so she has some idea of what's going on."

With a shrug, Saint sat back, a bit of an uncomfortable silence settling over the group. Harper held her breath waiting to see if anyone else would challenge her being there and was relieved when Banshee spoke up and drew them back to the business at hand.

"Okay, guys, I managed to hack into The Agency's server and find the file on Ex Nihilo."

"That's our team," Ryland reminded Harper.

"It contains all our personal information and, get this, it also has all of Merlin's info."

Beside her, Ryland sat up even straighter. The tension in the room escalated as everyone waited to find out who had thrown them to the wolves. Because a lot of their suspicions rested on him.

"Name?" Pharaoh asked.

"Cross Mills."

******

For a stunned moment, Ryland thought he heard Banshee wrong.

"That's not possible," Ryland said, gripping the edge of the table so hard it bit into his palms. The cross hanging around his neck seemed to burn into his skin.

"Who is Cross Mills?" Pharaoh asked.

Ryland couldn't process the conversation taking place and he had to force himself to say, "My dad. Well, his name is Nathan, but everyone always called him Cross, his SEAL nickname. But he died on a mission ten years ago."

"Are you sure about that?" Saint asked.

Fuck. Ryland swiped a hand through his messy hair, at a complete loss. There's no way his dad could be alive. He could still picture the notification team standing on their doorstep, asking permission to enter and waiting until he, his sister and mom sat down at the dining room table. It was all so solemn and formal. And when they delivered the news that his father had died on a classified mission, it felt like his world had imploded.

Although Ryland hadn't seen his dad much during those years after his parents separated, his dad had been his idol. Cross Mills had always appeared so big and strong. Larger than life. Undefeatable.

"Nathan 'Cross' Mills," Banshee said, typing away. "His records are sealed."

"He died on a classified mission," Ryland said

again, trying to process his thoughts and feeling a million miles away. He couldn't wrap his head around the idea that his dad might be alive. *Impossible.* They'd received his ashes.

Beside him, Harper laid a hand on his arm and he didn't pull away which caught him by surprise. Ryland wasn't used to leaning on anyone. Needing or receiving comfort was a foreign emotion for him. He was always the one running to everyone else's rescue. But Harper's touch told him she cared and empathized. That he wasn't alone. And he wasn't sure how he felt about that. The information overload was on the verge of frying his brain.

And, fuck! Could his dad really be alive?

"Address?" Pharaoh demanded.

"Somewhere on the Baja Peninsula."

"I'm going," Ryland stated.

"We're all going," Pharaoh amended. "Saint, get the GPS tracker off the Suburban. We're leaving in five."

Saint gave Pharaoh a salute, shoved back from the table and headed outside while everyone else stood to gather the gear they had with them.

Harper looked over at Ryland. "What about me?" she asked quietly, appearing unsure and hesitant.

"You're coming with us," he said, gaze raking

103

down her pajama-clad body. "Bruja, can you give Harper something to wear?" Though he had his go-to duffel bag, he imagined she'd rather wear something other than his clothes which would be much too large.

"Sure thing," Bruja answered and motioned for Harper to follow her.

******

The sun was coming up as the group hit the road and headed south from San Diego to cross the border into Mexico. Having gladly traded in her PJ's and pink slippers for some leggings and a t-shirt from Bruja, Harper sat beside Ryland and looked out at the dusty road and the desert landscape. They passed by a lot of rundown-looking shacks and several abandoned buildings as the sun worked its way higher and higher in the sky.

While Banshee drove, Pharaoh asked Ryland questions about his father. The closer they got, the more fidgety he seemed, playing with the silver chain around his neck as his knee bounced with nervous energy. The idea that his father might still be alive and working for The Agency was a huge curveball. Something none of them had anticipated.

"I just don't get it. If it's true—if he's still alive— why would he fake his death? How could he do that to us? And why is he hiding out in Mexico? Did he know I was a part of Ex Nihilo?"

He was talking in low tones, under his breath, directing his words to Harper only, but they were all listening. Once again, she found herself reaching over and laying a hand on his arm. She wanted to comfort him and every time she touched him, a jolt of awareness swept through her body.

"I wish I had answers for you. I can only imagine how shocked you are right now."

"We don't know anything for sure, though." Pharaoh drummed his fingers on the armrest. "This could be a wild goose chase."

"If he is alive, he's been up to some seriously secret shit," Saint said.

Looking around the SUV, Harper pulled in a breath and wondered what the hell she'd gotten herself into. She was surrounded by a serious group of badasses and she had so many questions. But she had a feeling she was on a need-to-know basis, and they apparently didn't think she needed to know much.

Clearly, they were some kind of black ops team and their job, as Ryland said, was to eliminate bad guys. A shiver ran through her as she considered exactly what that meant.

They killed people. For a living.

Swallowing hard, she studied Ryland's attractive

profile from beneath her lashes and wondered how many people he'd…murdered. Looks could be so deceiving. With his sun-bleached hair and easy grin, she'd always pegged him as carefree and harmless. Another SoCal surfer dude, carrying his board under his arm, and joking around.

But now she knew he was more than just a pretty boy. Her attention dropped from his tanned face—all high cheekbones and classic angles—down to his large hands and the tomahawk inked on his forearm. She remembered his calloused touch when they first shook hands. At the time, she had no idea what those hands were capable of and, now that she did, it was a little disconcerting. And, if she were being honest, it also thrilled her a little to know he could protect her if it ever came down to it.

The immense amount of training he probably received over the years gave her a sense of security. She assumed they were all former military so, despite how dangerous things might get, she knew she was in good hands. The very best.

Leaning back in the seat, Harper told herself not to worry. They'd figure out what was going on. She'd be back home in a day or two and this whole crazy adventure would feel like a dream.

That's what she kept trying to tell herself, anyway.

Chapter Nine

There was no way Ryland could contain the nerves fluttering through him as Banshee slowed the Suburban, parking under the shade of a palm tree. He had the door open before the SUV even came to a complete stop and was stalking up to the front door, ignoring Pharaoh who called out to him.

Was he being reckless? Absolutely. But he wanted answers. Deserved answers. If his father was still alive and had led Addie and him to believe otherwise for the past ten years...

He'd kill the bastard.

Ryland lifted his fist and started pounding as Harper and his team moved up beside him.

"Way to be subtle," Saint commented.

Ryland lifted his other hand and flipped him off. He wasn't in the mood for Saint's shit.

It seemed like he was knocking forever, but Ryland could've sworn he heard a muffled sound from inside. Looking up into the camera partially-concealed by the bright, climbing bougainvillea, he snapped, "Open the damn door before I break it down."

When the door slowly swung inward a couple of moments later, Ryland braced himself. His team had their hands on their guns, ready to spring into action, but Ryland wasn't worried about that kind of threat.

He did his best to hide his shock as a man stepped forward, the sunlight slanting across his face. Even though Nathan "Cross" Mills looked older, leaner and had a sweep of gray at his temples, there was no denying the truth.

His father was alive.

Holy. Fucking. Shit.

"Hi, son," Cross said, face emotionless as he eyed Ryland and the team standing on his doorstep. "I had a feeling this might happen."

"I don't fucking believe this," Ryland said, finally finding his voice.

With great reluctance, as though he knew he was in for a lot of questions, Cross pulled the door all the way open. "C'mon in. We have a lot to talk about."

"That's quite an understatement," Pharaoh said as everyone walked into the small, beachfront bungalow.

The windows were all open and a warm sea breeze blew inside as Ryland studied the man who left his life ten years ago. Hell, he didn't even know how to refer to him anymore. Dad? Father? Cross? The man was a virtual stranger. He also possessed a cool, calculating air that instantly put Ryland on guard.

Cross Mills wasn't the man he remembered. The one who regaled him with adventurous tales about being a SEAL. The one who taught him how to swim. The one who tucked him and Addie into bed when their mother was somewhere in Europe stealing some trinket.

Confusion swelled up inside him as he tried to come to terms with the situation. Ryland needed answers, but he had a feeling he wasn't going to hear what he wanted.

Cross led them over to the living room area and tossed some pillows aside to give them extra space to sit on the worn couch. "Sorry, but there isn't a lot of room." Harper made her way around the scarred coffee table to sit, but immediately stood again when nobody else joined her. "Please, sit, Miss—"

"Grant. Harper Grant."

"Right. Ryland's neighbor, I presume."

"You're the one who called and warned me. Didn't you?" Ryland eyed his father closely, and Cross nodded. "I don't understand. How the hell could you let us believe you were dead for the past ten years?"

Cross let out a resigned sigh. "I'm sorry, Ryland. Truly, I am. But an opportunity presented itself and I didn't have a choice."

"You always have a choice," Ryland snapped.

Cross studied his son. "There were so many times I wondered if I'd made the right decision. How I wish I could've been there when they pinned that Trident pin on you. You have no idea how proud I was."

Ignoring the emotions his father's words stirred, Ryland clamped his teeth together. It was so easy to say all that now, but the truth was he'd made a conscious decision to leave them. To disappear from their lives. And that hurt. "They gave us your ashes," Ryland gritted out.

"I know. I'm sorry." Cross raked a hand through his thick, sun-bleached hair which was so very much like his son's.

"Why did you do it?" He could feel his team's support as they all waited for an answer.

"I think that's a conversation for you and I to have later, in private. Right now, you need to understand

110

what's happening."

"Yeah, please," Saint said. "That would be nice."

"Did The Agency set us up to fail?" Pharaoh asked, crossing his large forearms. "Did they call for our termination?"

"It looks that way."

"Why?" Bruja asked.

Cross shrugged a shoulder. "I can't answer your questions. But I can tell you The Agency isn't what you think it is."

"Meaning what?" Banshee asked.

"Meaning they aren't the good guys. They are, in fact, very bad and extremely dangerous."

"How do you know?" Ryland asked, brow furrowed. "And why the hell should we believe anything you say?"

"You can believe whatever you want, but they lied to you. And to me. And I'm going to do everything in my power to make sure they implode because of it."

"Ok, let's start simple. Who the hell is The Agency exactly?" Pharaoh asked.

"A highly secret group with ties to the government. That's all I know."

"Then how do you know they're the bad guys?" Ryland pressed.

"They turned on you, their own team, didn't they?"

Although he had a point, Ryland couldn't fully believe the words coming out of his father's mouth. He had too many questions and way too many suspicions.

"What happened on that op?" Pharaoh asked, gray eyes stormy. "You're the one who gave us the mission parameters and then changed them at the last minute, *Merlin*."

"I merely followed the orders they gave me. By the time I realized you'd been set up, it was too late. The entire op turned into a clusterfuck and Tanner was dead. I'm sorry," he added in a low voice, eyes on Ryland. "I'd heard you two were close."

Ryland didn't bother to respond. He was doing his best to process the situation, but his skin felt itchy, his head throbbed, and it felt like the walls were closing in. He had so many questions and his father wasn't answering any of them. Fresh anger poured through him and it felt like his damn head was going to explode. His wild gaze searched for an exit, an escape from the chaos clamoring in his brain, and landed on the back sliding door.

In three long strides, Ryland reached the slider, threw it open and stepped onto the sand. He had no idea

112

where he was going or what he should believe. Sucking in a deep breath of fresh, salty air, he stalked away from the bungalow and headed down the beach, needing to get away from it all.

******

Harper didn't even think twice. She hurried after Ryland, determined to be there for him. The carefree, happy guy she'd first met was gone and in his place was someone hurting on a profound level. There was no missing the mistrust, confusion and betrayal flashing through his cobalt eyes. Maybe it was silly to go chasing him down the beach when she barely knew him. But her empathy ran deep and when she saw someone hurting, especially someone she cared about, she wanted to make it better.

Not too far ahead, Ryland dropped down on the sand, drew a leg up and propped his arm on it. Harper's nerves jangled as she reached him. Without a word, she sat down next to him. He didn't acknowledge her, just stared out at the ocean crashing along the shoreline.

Finally, he said, "I thought he died in a training accident. How could he let us believe that?"

The raw hurt in his voice made her chest tighten. Harper reached out and laid a hand on his arm. It seemed like she'd been doing that a lot lately, but it was the simplest, and safest, form of comfort she could offer. "For what it's worth, you're handling all of this like a rock star."

He let out a snort. "Hardly."

Turning to face him, tucking her legs beneath her, she squeezed his arm then released it. "You are. If my parents suddenly came back from the dead...well, I don't think I would've kept it together quite as well as you."

"It's just a huge shock. Addie is going to freak the fuck out."

"I mean, it's a good thing. You have your dad back."

"Do I?"

She tilted her head, not quite understanding. "What do you mean?"

"I don't know that man back there. He's a stranger and, for all I know, a liar."

"He's the one who called and warned you to go off grid. Because they were going to hunt your team down."

"Yeah. That's what he said." But there was no conviction in his tone.

"You don't believe him."

Ryland sighed. "I don't know what I believe anymore."

114

"Once you talk to him, maybe you'll get the answers you need."

"Maybe." Ryland pulled his attention off the waves and looked over at her. "I'm so damn sorry for dragging you into this mess."

"It's certainly been an adventure."

"I don't think the real adventure's even begun yet."

As she considered his words, she saw Cross slowly walking toward them. Almost as if he dreaded the conversation he knew he had to have with his son. When he reached them, Harper stood and placed a hand on Ryland's shoulder. This was something they needed to do in private.

"I'll see you in a bit," she said, and he gave a sharp nod.

******

As Ryland watched Harper walk away, his father sat down beside him and sighed.

"I'm not sure where to begin," Cross said.

"How about why you let us believe you died on some training mission?"

"I know you're not going to understand all of the choices I've made and I'm not asking you to. But you need to know that leaving you and your sister wasn't an easy decision."

"Why did you do it then?" Ryland couldn't hide the bitterness in his voice and wondered what had trumped him and Addie.

"It's a long story, but suffice it to say, I had reached a point in my military career where I needed more. When they offered it to me, I took it."

"Who's they?"

"The government," he said carefully.

Almost too easily? Ryland wondered. He shook his head in disgust, his anger and confusion building. "So you chose a job over your kids. Makes complete sense."

Fuck, he was mad. Curling his fingers into the sand, he squeezed hard and the grains slid through his white knuckles.

"Is that my necklace?" his dad asked, eyes on the silver cross around Ryland's neck.

Ryland tucked it back into his shirt. "Yeah. I've worn it since the day they delivered your ashes."

Cross had the decency to look chagrined, but he didn't comment. "And Addison? How is she?"

"Oh, Addie's terrific. You know, just continuing Mom's legacy—stealing antiquities and selling them off to rich assholes. You'd be proud."

"I never approved of your mother's occupation."

"You knowingly married a thief, Dad. Don't play innocent."

"I'm not perfect, Ryland, and I'm the first to admit I've made some questionable decisions. You better than anyone should understand that."

"What the fuck's that supposed to mean?" he snapped.

"Watch your tone."

Ryland let out a sharp bark of laughter. "Don't you dare try to act like a father now. You gave up that right when you left us thinking you were dead."

"Ryland—"

No, he'd had enough. "Just stop," Ryland gritted out and stood up. "I need to walk away now before I say something I'll regret."

Cross looked like he was going to comment further, but then shut his mouth. "Understood."

Stalking back across the beach, Ryland tried to get his emotions under control, but they were all over the place. His father wasn't answering his questions—not really—and he didn't think the man regretted any choice he'd made.

Including the shitty decision to leave him and

Addie.

Truthfully, the only thing Ryland wanted was an apology. A "sorry, kid, for choosing my career over you and letting you all think I was dead for the past ten years."

But, no, he didn't get that. And, as far as he could tell, he wasn't going to, either.

******

When Ryland returned to the bungalow, Harper could feel the intense anger rolling off him. He was seriously pissed and had every right to be angry at his father, but there was nothing she or his team could do. He'd have to make peace with his father on his own terms. Or maybe he never would. That was a decision only he could make.

But she could support him through it.

When he came over, she patted the place on the couch beside her. Without a word, he sat and ran a hand through his wild hair. His telltale move that told her he was frustrated.

A makeshift command center had already been set up and Banshee was typing furiously on his laptop. These guys did not mess around and were already working hard and digging for answers.

Crossing her legs, she silently thanked Bruja for the

wardrobe assistance. The badass woman was really growing on her. It didn't escape Harper's notice that her fellow male teammates respected her and treated her like an equal. At the same time, Harper also couldn't help but envy the woman's inherent beauty. Small but curvy, with thick, dark waves and light caramel eyes, she reminded her a little of a young Salma Hayek. She seemed like someone who could fit in anywhere. If this situation dragged out much longer, Harper hoped she could find a friend in the woman she was quickly coming to admire.

Thinking of women she admired, Harper still had to call Savannah, though she had no idea what she was allowed to say. *Sorry, Savvy, I'm on the run with a bunch of former military guys turned assassins and there's some secret group trying to kill us all. So, we'll be off grid for the foreseeable future.*

Off grid. It was definitely a term she never expected to use when referring to herself. Harper would laugh if the situation wasn't so serious. Suddenly, she'd been dropped into the middle of a *Mission: Impossible* flick and had no idea what to expect next.

The rear sliding door opened and Ryland tensed beside her when his father walked inside. The air immediately changed and became a little more reserved, slightly heavier. Definitely more frigid. Cross seemed to have a knack for putting them all on edge.

"Have you found anything?" Cross asked Banshee,

moving closer and trying to get a look at his computer screen.

"Still working on it." Banshee turned sideways in his chair, subtly blocking the other man's view.

"The Agency called for Ex Nihilo's immediate termination," Cross said, eyeing the team. "They didn't give me a reason, and they can't find out I warned you."

He almost sounded nervous, and Harper glanced over at Ryland who narrowed his eyes, but didn't comment.

"Wouldn't they assume you'd warn your son?" Bruja glanced from one to the other.

"No."

"And why's that?" Pharaoh asked.

"Because I always put the mission first," Cross stated coolly. "It's what we're trained to do."

His cold words pierced Harper's heart like an arrow. "What an asshole thing to say," she blurted out, unable to stop herself. Maybe she should shut up and keep her comments to herself, but Cross just stepped over the line. Beside her, Ryland sat up a little taller and she swore she felt his approval.

"I'm sorry if you disagree with me, Miss Grant. I wouldn't expect you to understand."

Harper narrowed her eyes. "I would say this is none of my business, but seeing as I've been dragged into it, I think I should be allowed to weigh in. And, in my humble opinion, your family, whether it's your team or your blood, should always be first. Period. Not some mission."

"Hooyah," Ryland said, sending a glare in his father's direction. "SEALs don't leave anyone on their team behind. Ever. Maybe you forgot that."

"Hooyah," Banshee echoed.

"Army doesn't either," Pharaoh stated, gray eyes flashing silver lightning.

"No, it doesn't," Bruja added.

They all had just revealed a large chunk of their past and Harper knew that was huge. All gazes turned to Saint who remained quiet.

"Can't say the same for the FSS. Fuckers tried to kill me multiple times." Saint shrugged. "Shame, too, cuz I'm such a likable guy."

"I knew it!" Banshee declared. "I had you pegged for Russian Intelligence."

"It's not something I talk about," he said, clamming up fast. "So don't ever ask me about it."

"I haven't forgotten anything about being a SEAL," Cross said, voice tinged in annoyance. "And we're not

121

dealing with the military. We're dealing with a covert group who plays by their own rules of engagement. So, you either learn to check your conscience at the door and carry out the job or they remove you from the situation. Permanently. It's just a fact."

A muscle flexed in Ryland's cheek, but he didn't reply.

"Now, if you're ready to listen, I've got some advice." No one said anything, just waited for Cross to continue. "The Agency is an evil group who isn't targeting just bad guys. They're about self-interest and self-preservation. If something or someone no longer serves them, they wind up on their kill list. Apparently, Ex Nihilo, for whatever reason, wasn't serving them any longer."

Ryland and his team exchanged looks.

"So, that means you've got two options," Cross continued. "One, go off grid permanently, assume a new identity and hope they don't hunt you down. Or, two, eliminate The Agency. But you each have to make your own decision and understand you'll more than likely end up like Tanner."

Cross's words hung heavy in the air for a long moment.

Ryland leaned forward in his seat. "I'm going to do everything in my power to bring down the fuckers who killed Tanner," he swore, and Harper shivered.

Chapter Ten

It had been a long day and the sun was beginning to set over the Pacific Ocean. Ryland was still trying to sort out everything in his head, but he knew one thing for certain: he was incredibly grateful to have Harper by his side. Her mere presence somehow made everything a little better. He wasn't sure how or why, but she steadied him.

Ryland and Harper told the team they were going for a walk, and they stopped a little way up the beach from his father's bungalow. Now, they were sitting side by side under a palm tree, and he couldn't tear his eyes off her. Her blonde hair shimmered like gold in the setting sun and when she turned to look up at him, her aqua eyes sparkled, outshining the sea itself. He focused on her adorable freckles and, like always, imagined kissing each one.

More than anything, he wanted—needed—to put his father out of his mind because his personal shit was clouding his thoughts. Making him not as focused on The Agency as he should be. And he needed to take them down. For Tanner.

And for the woman beside him. Harper was a beautiful distraction he'd been longing to get to know better for the past month. The tropical paradise all around them was magical and he wished they were on vacation instead of on the run, but he wasn't about to let another opportunity pass him by.

"I'm sorry our date didn't happen, but I'm pretty sure we would've gone out on a second one."

"And a third one?" Harper asked with a lopsided smile.

Ryland reached out, unable to stop himself, and laid a hand along the side of her face. "And a fourth and a fifth." She leaned her cheek into his palm and his attention dropped to her lips. "I think this is a little overdue."

Lowering his head, Ryland captured her mouth with his, intending to keep their first kiss easy and gentle. But the passion he'd been holding in check burst like a dam the moment her lips parted in invitation. He swept his tongue into her mouth and she instantly met him, stroke for stroke, as they explored and teased.

Harper Grant tasted sweeter than he imagined she would, and he slid his hand into her wavy hair, threading his fingers through its softness, tilting her head back and deepening the kiss. He hadn't hooked up with anyone since he started working with The Agency and, damn, his neglected dick was aching for more.

Maybe it wasn't the time or place, or maybe it was the perfect moment, but Ryland pushed Harper back into the sand and kissed her thoroughly. Her hands circled around his neck, dragging him down with her, then sank into his unruly hair. There's no way she could miss his stiff length digging into her hip. He wanted her badly—had since day one—so she may as well know it.

Never one to play games when he liked a woman, Ryland always made his intentions clear. If he got lucky, great. If he didn't, he moved on to greener pastures. And he always made it known that whatever happened, it would be fleeting. Long-term wasn't in his vocabulary due to his work and the time he spent away on missions. Clingy women were instant red flags and made him run in the opposite direction.

But Harper was different. For the first time in his life, Ryland wondered what it would be like to call this gorgeous, intelligent and amazing woman his girlfriend. His woman. *All mine.* The thought made him grow harder.

Yeah, he liked that idea a lot.

He thought about how quickly she'd offered up her sister's restaurant, giving them all a temporary safe harbor in a chaotic storm she never could have anticipated. How in tune she was to his emotions, always quick to offer a reassuring touch or word. About the way she'd boldly stood up for him to his father. Yeah, she was different. And he really liked that.

Ryland kissed his way along her jawline and down her soft neck, alternating between licking and nipping. Why did she taste so sweet? And that vanilla scent of hers, now tinged with coconut, was driving him crazy. When she whimpered softly and tilted her head sideways to give him better access, he knew he had to rein it in or he'd lose control. And she deserved more than a quick fuck on the beach. Besides, he hated sand and all the potential crevices it could get caught in. Screwing on the beach wasn't all it was cracked up to be.

Forcing himself to pull back, Ryland looked down into her passion-glazed eyes and his mouth edged up. Yeah, she wanted him just as badly as he wanted her. His brain told him to get up and move away, but that was easier said than done. The heat between them was scorching and the way those sexy, aqua eyes of hers slow-blinked up at him gave him no choice. He slammed his mouth back down against hers and kissed the shit out of her. It was all tongue and teeth and desperation.

Nearby, a throat cleared and Ryland reluctantly broke the steamy kiss, looking up to see his father mere feet away. Annoyed, he sighed and rolled away from Harper who quickly sat up, cheeks flushed and turning even redder with embarrassment.

"We need to talk," Cross said, all business. When Harper moved to get up, he raised a hand. "Stay. This involves you, too."

As she sank back down in the sand next to him, Ryland silently cursed his father to hell for his rotten timing. He'd been MIA for the past ten years, dead to everyone who knew him, and he shows up now when Ryland was finally connecting with the girl of his dreams.

Seriously great fucking timing, Dad.

******

Cross sat down across from Ryland and Harper, and she couldn't look his father in the eye. Hell, he'd just caught them writhing around in the sand like a couple of horny teenagers. Her heart was still pounding madly and her body was hot and needy. Shifting her legs, squeezing her thighs together, she tried not to think about how wet her panties were.

She had been ready to leave, make her escape, when Cross told her to stay. Now she was stuck there and had no idea what he wanted. But she knew she didn't like the man. He hadn't chosen his family. Had abandoned them. Walked away from Ryland, his only son, for a job. And despite having only spent a little over twenty-four hours together, she already knew she would choose Ryland every time.

"I want to make sure you understand the gravity of the situation." Cross's words carried a lot of weight, his voice deep and commanding. When Harper finally looked up, feeling steady enough to look him in the eye, she found his steely gaze focused on her. He had the same cobalt-colored eyes as Ryland but, somehow, they were different. Harder, colder. Ryland had a playfulness in his that Cross was lacking.

Harper waited for him to continue.

"If you want to bring down The Agency, that needs to be your only goal—your life—until they're defeated. Do you understand?"

Harper frowned. No, actually, she didn't understand. "You make it sound like I can't go home."

"You can't," Cross stated firmly.

"What?" She glanced over at Ryland who remained quiet, but she could sense him silently seething at her father. Was it because of what he'd said? Or because he knew his father was right? "What about my sister? I have to call her. And my apartment. And what about Betty? I can't just disappear!" The moment the words left her mouth, Harper realized how pathetic they sounded. With her lack of family and friends, she was technically the perfect candidate to disappear and no one would even know. Well, except for Savvy.

The reality check of how very empty her life was nearly knocked the wind out of her.

"You're going to need to cut ties with everyone in your life," Cross told her.

Harper shook her head, eyes narrowing at the man. "No. What about my—"

"This isn't about you!" Cross snapped.

"Dad," Ryland growled out a warning, "leave her alone. Let me handle it."

"Because you've been handling the situation so well?" he asked, sarcasm rolling over each word. Cross pulled in a breath, reeling in his anger before continuing more calmly. "Listen to me, Miss Grant. Despite you being a distraction…" he looked over at Ryland, "if you go back home now, you will not only put yourself in danger, but also everyone you love. The people you're dealing with are ruthless and will not hesitate to slit your throat in the middle of the night. Then they'll do the same to your sister."

The idea of dragging Savannah into this mess and possibly her getting hurt, or worse, wasn't an option. But what if she never saw her again? Tears pricked Harper's eyes. "Can I at least talk to her and explain what's happening?"

"That wouldn't be wise."

Squeezing her hands into fists, forcing the tears back, Harper muttered, "Excuse me," and hurried away. Her feet couldn't carry her away fast enough as the tears broke free, sliding down her cheeks. But there was no running from the problem. She'd been sucked into an absolute shit show, complete with assassins and an evil, clandestine organization. It truly was the plot of some crazy movie.

Except she was living it.

"Harper!"

The sound of Ryland's voice made her pause and he easily caught up. Of all the apartment complexes in all of San Diego, she'd chosen the one where Ryland Mills lived. And she'd simply thought he was just some good-looking, laid-back surfer with a charming smile and easy going nature. But the harmless wave rider turned out to be a secret assassin.

In what world did this happen?

Harper swiped at her eyes and stopped walking, but she couldn't look up at Ryland. Her thoughts were in turmoil and frustration filled her.

Ryland reached out, lifted her chin with his finger and said, "Let's call your sister."

******

Hell, it was the least he could for dragging her into this clusterfuck. And if his father didn't like it, he could go fuck himself. Harper was just a civilian. She never signed up for this shit. She'd also made it clear Savannah was the only important person she had in her life.

"Really?" Her tear-bright eyes glittered so brightly with hope, Ryland's chest tightened. He'd made her cry. This whole damn thing was his fault and he felt awful. All he wanted to do was fix things, and if that meant sneaking a call then that's what he would do.

"Really," he said. "C'mon."

Leading her back to the bungalow, he found Banshee in the corner, feet propped up, computer on his lap and chomping on a bowl of freshly-cut mango. "You gotta try this. Juiciest mango I've ever had."

"I don't like mango," Ryland said and looked over at Harper, arching a dark brow. "Want some?"

"No thanks," she murmured. "I prefer pineapple."

"Me too," Ryland agreed.

"There's a pineapple plant in the front yard," Banshee told them. "And just about every other tropical fruit, too."

"Great, but I need a favor first," Ryland said, lowering his voice.

"You're always using me. I'm beginning to question our friendship." Banshee fake-pouted, popping another piece of mango into his mouth.

"I need your hacking skills. Can you set up a secure line so Harper can call her sister?"

Banshee dropped his feet and sat up straighter. "Is that a good idea?"

"No, but it's necessary. So we need to make sure it can't be traced and we keep it on the down low. Think you can handle it?"

Banshee stifled a huff of indignation. "Are you questioning my abilities?"

"Not at all." Ryland grinned and Banshee gave him a nod.

"Alright. Where do we want to set up?"

"How about the bedroom?"

"Sure thing." Banshee set the bowl of mango aside and stood up. "Gimme five minutes."

"Thanks, Banshee. I owe you."

"Yeah, I know. You owe me a lot," he said as he walked away.

"He can get grumpy," Ryland explained with a shrug. "But he always comes through."

Harper sent him a grateful smile. "Thank you for helping me."

"You're welcome." The happiness and relief on her face was worth the ass-reaming he'd get if his father found out. "Who's Betty?"

"My fish," she murmured.

"Ah, I see. Don't worry. We'll make sure your sister knows to take care of Betty."

The smile she gave him was pure gratitude and relief, and his entire world seemed to light up.

It took Banshee half as long as he said and, in less than three minutes, Harper was talking to Savannah through a video call on Banshee's laptop.

"Ohmygod, Harper," Savannah exclaimed. "I've been texting and calling all day! Where are you?"

Both Ryland and Banshee stayed off-camera, but Ryland peered over the top of the monitor and got his first look at Savannah Grant. She had the same blonde hair as Harper, but shorter, sweeping the tops of her shoulders, and instead of bright blue eyes, hers were a smoky sage.

"Um, well, I can't say exactly, but I wanted you to know I'm safe."

"What do you mean you can't say?"

"FYI, you've got three minutes," Banshee stated. "Then the call disconnects."

"Who is that?" Savannah demanded.

"Savvy, listen to me. I don't want you to worry, but I'm going to be away for a little while. I can't tell you any details…" she looked up at Ryland and he nodded, "but can you feed Betty while I'm gone? Maybe take her back to your place so she isn't alone? She likes when you talk to her, too."

"Yes, I'll watch your fish but, Harper, are you really okay?"

"I am and I promise to call you again when I can. Sorry for being so mysterious, but I have to be."

"Does this have anything to do with the neighbor you had a date with? The one who's a spy or something?"

Hovering above the monitor, Ryland tilted his head, wondering just how many times Harper had mentioned him to her sister, but shook it in an emphatic no.

"Um, I…" She hesitated over her next words, eventually deciding not to acknowledge her sister's reference to him. It was a good choice on Harper's part— the less Savannah knew, the better—and relieved a bit of the tension over how much she might accidentally give away through their conversation. "I swear I'm fine. Just please take care of Betty and I'll be in touch, okay?"

Savannah gave a long sigh. "Okay," she finally relented.

"Love you, sis."

"Love you, too."

The call ended and Ryland met Harper's grateful eyes. "Thank you," she mouthed and sent him a stunning smile. His heart felt a little lighter, a lot more full, and he vowed to do just about anything to keep her smiling like that.

Chapter Eleven

After talking to her sister, Harper felt better. At least until Cross returned and launched back into his "discussion" of them going off grid. And this time pulling the entire team into the conversation.

"For how long?" Harper interrupted when she couldn't take their back and forth anymore. She couldn't help it and needed a more clear-cut answer of how long she'd have to stay away from home. Basically be on the run. "A week? Two weeks?" Maybe she shouldn't be so worried about it, relax and let the professionals handle it. But a part of her was scared she wouldn't like the answer she was about to get.

And she was right.

"Indefinitely," Cross answered vaguely. His blue eyes focused on her like lasers, and she shifted beneath their intensity. "There is another option, though."

"What?" Pharaoh asked.

"Make The Agency believe you're dead and no longer a threat."

"Fake our own deaths?" Bruja asked. "Doesn't that seem extreme?"

"That seems like a last resort," Ryland said, watching Harper's reaction closely. "Why not just assume new identities? It's not like we don't have someone who can whip some of those up." She followed his eyes back to Banshee.

"Maybe I didn't make myself clear before," Cross snapped. "You all have targets on your backs and they won't stop until you're dead. So if I sound like I'm being extreme, it's because the situation is FPCON Delta. Get it?"

Harper frowned. Tempers were escalating again, and she had no idea what FPCON Delta even meant— and why it was so bad—until Ryland explained, "Force Protection Delta is the highest state of alert issued by the DoD for a known threat."

"That's why we're going to take the threat out," Saint stated. He slid a look in Harper's direction. "It's what we do."

A shiver ran down Harper's spine. "What if you

138

can't find them? How will you stop them?"

"We'll find them," Banshee said confidently. "I've got programs running and it's only a matter of time before I get some intel to help us move forward."

"It could take months. Even years," Cross commented.

"Way to be positive," Bruja scoffed.

"Years?" Harper exclaimed in disbelief. "So what're you saying? I might never see my sister again?"

"It's a possibility."

"Dad, please. Jesus." Ryland scrubbed a hand over his stubbled jaw. "Harper, we'll have answers soon and, I promise you, we'll take care of the situation and you'll get to go home sooner rather than later."

"Don't lie to her," Cross said.

"I'm not," Ryland gritted out between his clamped teeth.

For a long, very uncomfortable moment, father and son stared off. Then, Cross relented and said, "Consider yourself warned."

Worry filled Harper, but she chose to believe Ryland over his father. She didn't trust Cross as far as she could throw him, and something about him set her on edge. If anyone was lying, her money was on him. After all, he was the one who let his family believe he died.

"We need a game plan," Pharaoh announced. "And a place to stay. Ideally, a place that can serve as a base of operations with enough room to sleep. Any ideas?" He looked over at Cross who nodded.

"There's an abandoned warehouse about ten minutes from here," Cross offered. "It's set back from the road and would be a perfect place for you to set up shop."

"Let's check it out." Ryland stood up.

Harper could tell he was itching to get out of there and, to be honest, so was she. Something about the whole situation felt off, but she couldn't quite place her finger on it. As she was trying to figure it out, Banshee's laptop began beeping and he glanced down at the screen.

"Hold onto your hats, kids, because I just hit the jackpot."

All attention turned to Banshee who was grinning like the Cheshire Cat.

"What do you got?" Pharaoh asked.

"Your boy just uncovered a list of people who sit on The Agency throne."

"Fuck yeah," Ryland murmured, and they all exchanged grins.

"You're certain it's The Agency?" Cross asked,

leaning forward.

"First, never doubt my hacking abilities. And second, hell yeah, I'm sure. Only problem is the file's encrypted, so I'm going to need to work on it a little more."

"We have our hit list, boys." Saint tilted his neck and it cracked.

Pharaoh stood. "Banshee, you keep working on it. Bruja, stay with him. The rest of us will go check out that warehouse."

******

It didn't take long to reach the abandoned warehouse. The place was big and open with a lot of space, but filthy. It had obviously been empty for a while and the elements had taken over. It was remote, but not exactly move-in ready. Yes, they'd all—well almost all—been in worse places during their careers, but they would lose valuable time just making it usable.

While they surveyed the space, trying to decide where to start setting up and cleaning, Ryland placed his hands on his hips and frowned. "We can't sleep here with the rats," he stated, pulling out his phone to send his father a quick *what-the-fuck* message.

"You wanna go find us somewhere else?" Saint asked. "Because I'd rather go sleep on the beach with the

141

sand fleas than spend the night in this shit hole. It's worse than a Russian Gulag."

"What would you know about a Russian prison?" Pharaoh asked.

"More than I'd like," Saint mumbled.

Ryland slapped a hand on Saint's back. "I'll find us some better digs. Scrounge up some food, too. You guys start cleaning. Just in case." It had been a long twenty-four hours and Ryland knew Harper must be exhausted. He and his team could go for a while and run on fumes, if necessary, but she was different. And he would make sure she was taken care of and not hungry, thirsty and forced to sleep in some rodent-infested pile of crap.

No. Not his Harper. She deserved better than that.

His Harper.

The possessive thought made him pause, but he couldn't deny it. He wanted her, all of her, and after those scorching kisses they shared earlier, Ryland needed more. For the first time in his life, it was more than just a physical want, though. He enjoyed talking to her, listening to her and getting to know her better. Just looking into her aqua eyes did something funny to his insides.

Fuck. She gave him all the feels. And he liked it.

Ryland and Harper got in the Suburban and

followed the road to the first of three addresses his father sent in reply to his message. Apparently, Cross owned three more bungalows that he claimed to rent out to tourists for extra cash. *Nice of him to offer those up to begin with*, Ryland thought, barely containing an eyeroll as they approached the location.

The bungalows were separated a decent distance apart so they had some privacy, but were also within a football's throw of each other. They were a little dusty inside, but the pantries were stocked with dry foods and would serve well enough for tonight. Besides, it was getting late and it's not like they could just order a pizza. They were in the middle of nowhere.

While Ryland called the others and told them about the setup, Harper found a box of macaroni and cheese. She boiled the noodles and was dumping the orange powder in the saucepan by the time Ryland disconnected his call to Pharaoh.

"They're on their way," Ryland said and sat down at the small kitchen table. "Pharaoh and Saint will be next door and Banshee and Bruja will be on the other side of them."

"And I'll be with you?" Harper asked, voice teasing as she set a bowl in front of Ryland.

"Damn straight," Ryland answered and dug into the mac and cheese. He groaned, not realizing just how hungry he was, and the cheap crap really hit the spot. "I don't think a ninety-nine cent box of powdered mac and cheese ever tasted so good."

"I added some salt," she said with a smile and took a bite.

For a long moment they ate in silence while Ryland contemplated their sleeping arrangements. There was nothing he wanted more than Harper in bed with him, but he knew his ass would be on the stiff rattan couch with an even stiffer dick. But he'd suffer in silence because jumping Harper was off the table.

Tonight, anyway.

Tomorrow was a whole new day with brand new opportunities. And if they were being hunted down, he wasn't going to turn down the chance of being with Harper if the situation presented itself.

******

The idea that a group of people were currently hunting them down terrified Harper, and Ryland's earlier kisses on the beach left her libido in a tizzy. Her mind was buzzing with so many unanswered questions. It was all coming together to create a whirlwind of conflicting thoughts and feelings.

What if Cross was right? What if her time on this Earth was coming to a close and there was nothing she could do about it? Normally, she was a pretty optimistic person and Savannah was the realist. But, in this case, she didn't want to waste a moment of time.

Especially if it was running out.

And with Ryland so close to her...well, not taking advantage of that fact would be a straight up shame. She didn't want to die with regrets and the former SEAL fascinated her.

After scarfing down the quick meal she'd made, Ryland told her to shower first. She'd dug her pajamas out of his go-to duffel bag he'd packed them in earlier and now she sat on the bed in the small one-bedroom bungalow, nervously worrying her lower lip and contemplating her next move. She was pretty sure Ryland wanted her the way she wanted him, but he definitely seemed to be holding back. Was it more gentlemanly behavior? And how could she convince him it was okay for him to let that all go?

After Patrick had shredded what little self-esteem she had when it came to sex, she was beginning to seriously doubt herself. But then she remembered the way Ryland had kissed her earlier. No one had ever devoured her like that before and it turned her on like crazy.

That little voice of doubt in her head was chattering away, though, and she couldn't help but fear she was more attracted to him than he was to her. And if that were the case then she'd crawl outside and bury her head in the sand.

So humiliating. Like Patrick all over again, telling her that their sex life had left him wanting and disappointed.

Harper dragged her hands over her face and sighed heavily. Maybe this was a horrible idea and it would be better if she just forgot about—

"Hey." Ryland's soft voice interrupted her thoughts. He stood in the doorway, a towel loosely wrapped around his narrow hips.

Harper couldn't help it. She openly stared, unable to stop her mouth from opening. A broad chest, strong shoulders, narrow waist. Those delicious indentations that created a V. Her eyes zeroed in on a water droplet as it slid down his firm torso and got lost in a groove of his insane six-pack abs. The urge to find that lone drop and lick it away had her fisting the comforter.

Forcing her gaze back up, Harper tried to ignore her pulse thundering in her ears.

His lips twitched as he said, "I forgot my clothes."

And that was fine with her. She nodded, unable to find her voice, and he walked in, bent over and unzipped his duffel bag.

Holy hotness. Harper dropped her head back, eyes fixed on the ceiling, and silently mouthed, "Oh. My.

146

God."

All that chiseled perfection left her head spinning. She was at a complete loss. Thoughts of seduction flew out the window because the idea of being with a man like that—a freaking Adonis—made her so nervous, her throat went dry and her palms started sweating.

Patrick's slightly below-average body looked nothing like Ryland Mills. And if she hadn't been good enough for Patrick, how in the world would she be able to please the sun-bronzed god standing before her.

Pulling her eyes off his tight ass, Harper tried not to drool as Ryland stood back up and turned around. His cobalt eyes met hers and she swore they were filled with amusement. "Mind if I borrow a blanket?"

"N-no. Of course not." Sliding off the bed, she grabbed the bedspread she'd been sitting on and handed it to him.

"Thanks." He took it and tilted his head. "Are you okay?"

Every once in a while, for whatever reason, a situation came along that made Harper so nervous she'd start talking and not be able to stop. It didn't happen often, but she could feel the babble bubbling up and there wasn't a thing she could do as the word vomit spilled from her mouth.

"I feel bad making you sleep on the couch," she began, twisting her hands. "It looks really uncomfortable and way too short for your long legs. You look even taller than usual. Which is weird because I mean, I know you're tall. Probably what? Six two or three? I'm only five three which is so short, but that's why there are heels right? My sister, Savannah, she's taller than me and—"

"Harper," he interrupted. She immediately shut up and was on the verge of crawling out the door and burying her runaway mouth in the sand when he reached out and laid a finger over her lips. "Breathe, sweetheart."

Her lips parted, she sucked in a breath and, without thinking, wrapped her lips around his finger. Seemingly of its own accord, her tongue swirled around the tip as she sucked lightly.

All traces of humor left his face and fierce need took its place as he pulled in a sharp breath. He dropped the blanket and gripped her hip, fingers digging into her skin.

Reality came crashing back and Harper released his finger with a pop and swallowed hard. "I'm sorry," she whispered, trying to bring her brain back on-line to make a quick escape. She began to pull back, but he grabbed her, dragging her body forward.

"Don't you dare be sorry for doing the sexiest damn thing I've ever seen," he ordered huskily. He slid his other hand through her hair, gaze searching hers. "Why

148

are you so jumpy?"

"Because—" Her voice faltered. "I mean, look at you."

"Look at *you*," he countered. "I'm the one who's nervous as hell."

A frown appeared between her brows. "You?"

"Sweetheart, you are the most beautiful woman I've ever laid eyes on and right now I'm committed to sleeping on that godawful couch so I don't push things too far and chase you away. Now tell me, what's going on in that pretty head of yours?"

Okay, here was her big chance. Gathering her courage, Harper let go of her anxiety and threw caution to the wind. "I want you to stay here with me. If we're running out of time, I want this night with you, Ryland."

Chapter Twelve

Ryland stood there, studying her in silence for the briefest moment. Then he yanked Harper against his damp skin and his mouth crashed against hers, consuming it with an unrelenting passion she'd never felt from a man before. It was even hotter than the kiss on the beach. Probably because only a thin towel separated their bodies.

After what felt like forever, they broke apart, panting. "Don't you dare doubt how badly I want you," Ryland murmured, tugging her even closer so she couldn't miss his rock-hard arousal pressing into her belly.

The towel didn't conceal much and Harper let her hands skim over his firm chest. "Sorry. Just stupid hang ups from my last relationship that I can't seem to shake." But that was the last thing she wanted to discuss. *Time to deflect.* Her fingers touched the cross hanging around his neck. "Are you religious?"

"No. It was my dad's," he told her then frowned. "What hang ups?"

She hesitated. He didn't want to discuss his father and she didn't want to discuss Patrick. Instead of remaining at a stalemate, she attempted to gather her courage and open up. "When he broke up with me, he said..." *Dammit.* She didn't want to talk about Patrick and when she started to pull away, Ryland held her in place.

"Uh-uh. Tell me what your assclown of an ex said."

Harper let out a soft sigh. "He said he wasn't attracted to me and the sex wasn't enough of a reason to stay because it was only okay and I wasn't very good at...things. I could never...relax." She squeezed her eyes shut, unable to believe she just babbled out her biggest humiliation. "But I was under too much stress and when he kicked me out—"

"He kicked you out?" His words were sharp, gritted through clenched teeth.

"Yeah, I'd been staying at his place for a few weeks after losing my apartment. But then he got a new girlfriend." She really didn't want to get into the dirty details, but Ryland didn't let it drop.

"And then you moved to San Diego to be near your sister?"

"No. I should've, but I made a promise to myself that I'd stick it out and pursue acting." She gave a sad chuckle. "But I just became another sad Hollywood statistic, living in my car."

"Living in your—" He stopped mid-sentence and a muscle ticked in his jaw. "You had nowhere to live and that fucker threw you out?"

The fierceness in his voice caught her by surprise. The last thing she meant to do was unload her shitty past year on him. He had enough to worry about. "Can we not talk about it, please?"

Ryland swore under his breath. "Listen to me, Harper. First, I want you to forget all about that dickwad and never waste another thought on anything he said or did. And second…" He took her hand and slowly dragged it down, down, down. She froze when he placed her hand over his raging erection. His voice came out raspy when he said, "I have full faith that you are very good at all the things."

God, he was so big and hard as steel. Her breath caught in her throat and her confidence wavered. "I'm scared I'll disappoint you," she whispered.

"Impossible." He leaned in and kissed her. It was gentle, extremely tender, and when she opened her mouth

152

for more, he stepped back. "Why don't you let me take care of you tonight? Show you exactly how wrong you are to believe anything he said."

She wasn't exactly sure what he meant, but when he extended his hand, she didn't hesitate to lay hers in his. His warm fingers wrapped around hers and tugged her over to the bed. "Sit," he ordered, eyeing her like his next meal.

Harper lowered herself onto the edge of the bed, trying not to let her insecurities hold her back. Ryland slid his hands over her tense shoulders and squeezed. Then he motioned for her to scoot back, and the mattress sank as he joined her.

"On your belly, sweetheart," he said, twirling his fingers in a circle.

"My belly?" she echoed.

"I'm taking care of you tonight. Starting with a massage."

With a small nod, Harper rolled onto her stomach and Ryland moved over her, locking her in with his knees. She knew that towel was stretched wide and probably falling off him and that sent a surge of heat straight down between her thighs.

Ryland's large hands began to rub and knead, working the tension from her shoulders, and in minutes, she was sighing softly. God, his hands were magic. "How are you so good at this?" she murmured, cheek against the cool sheets. She felt like she was sinking into the bed, all of her stress, inhibitions and anxiety melting away from his soothing touch.

"I'm good at quite a few things," he answered, and she heard the smile in his voice.

"Mmm, don't ever stop."

"How about we try something else?" he suggested.

He swept her long hair aside and when his lips touched the back of her neck, she moaned softly. They were so soft and when he began kissing and licking her skin, a shuddering breath escaped her lungs.

"You taste so sweet, Harper." His hands slid under her shirt and played with the waistband of her shorts. "Do you taste this sweet everywhere?"

Words escaped her as his hand curved over her ass and squeezed.

"I have a feeling you do," he murmured, voice low and sexy in her ear.

Goosebumps pricked her skin and, with her head still turned sideways, she saw his towel fly through the air and land in a pile on the floor. Knowing Ryland was naked and straddling her, touching her and whispering naughty things in her ear, had Harper breathing harder.

154

Her heart started galloping and the anticipation of what he would do next had her fisting the sheets.

Her previous nerves dissolved and all she wanted was his hands and mouth all over her. As if he heard her thoughts, Ryland did exactly that. He lifted her shirt and slowly kissed his way down her spine, spending extra time at the two indentations on her lower back.

"So damn sexy." His low, husky voice sent her stomach fluttering. After thoroughly licking her lower back dimples, he spent an inordinate amount of time tracing his tongue in slow circles above the edge of her pajama bottoms and then proceeded lower, dragging his hands over her ass and leaving light butterfly kisses along the backs of her thighs.

He kept scooching backwards and when she started to turn over, he pressed a firm hand against her lower back. "Nope. Stay put, sweetheart. I'm not done yet. Not even close."

Swallowing hard, Harper lowered her face back down to the bed and waited to see what he would do next. His hands caressed along her sides, over her hips and then dipped between her legs. *Oh, God.* Those calloused fingers slid up her inner thigh, disappeared in her shorts and skimmed over the seam of her panties. Light strokes, up and down, and her eyes fluttered shut.

Hot need began building and she bit her lip when he slid his other hand underneath her body and hiked her up just a bit, giving him better access. His hand moved around, slid down the front of her panties and his fingers found her clit. He pressed on the bundle of nerves, teasing and massaging until she began whimpering.

Harper's hands twisted the sheets and she arched up as he slid a finger into her wet core. Her body tightened around it, her hips rocking, and she moaned softly.

"Feeling better?" he asked, voice rough with need.

Hell, yes! she wanted to scream. Better than she'd ever felt before. But words escaped her and she could only answer with an incoherent mumble of satisfaction.

Suddenly, Ryland jerked her panties and shorts off and lifted her up onto her knees, holding her back against his front. His body was hard and warm, and he held her in place with one hand and sank a second finger in her pulsating core. His thumb circled her clit, finding the perfect pressure and rhythm, until she was gasping and bucking against his hand.

"That's right. Ride it, sweetheart. Don't hold back." His mouth was at her ear, voice low, breath warm and pepperminty. "Let go. I want to hear the sounds you make when you come."

"Oh, God…" Harper's head dropped back against his shoulder and the orgasm slammed into her, hard and fast, like it never had before. She cried out, her entire body stiffening, then went limp in his arms. She would've fallen over like a ragdoll if he hadn't kept her propped up against his solid chest.

Pressing his lips to her temple, he pulled his fingers out of her wet passage and let her slide down. Twisting around onto her back, she looked up at Ryland who hovered above her on his knees. His massive cock looked ready to blow and was so close she could see every detail.

She had never cared to get too close to one before and giving head was something she avoided. It made her gag. But the sight of Ryland's impressive cock was making her mouth water and she wondered just how much of it she could fit in her mouth.

Heart thundering and head filled with dirty thoughts, she watched Ryland lift his fingers and suck her juices off. And she nearly orgasmed again.

"So fucking sweet," he said, voice strained and husky. "Just like I knew you'd be."

Harper was speechless. No one had ever spoken to her like that and she'd never experienced this level of intimacy before. Holy hell, it was such a turn-on.

When she reached up to touch his cock, he backed away. "I'm not done with you," Ryland growled. He moved faster than she expected and scooped her ass up off the mattress, burying his face between her thighs.

"Ryland," she gasped, trying to twist away. He

responded by tossing her legs over his shoulders. His grip was firm and his mouth was latched onto her pussy like a damn vacuum attachment, sucking the holy bejesus out of her. Tonguing her into another orgasm in less than a minute. Something she thought would've been an impossible feat.

Screaming, Harper squeezed her thighs against his head, and saw stars. Her fingers threaded through the long, sun-bleached hair on top of his head and her soft cries echoed through the room as indescribable pleasure rolled over her, blasting her to heights she never imagined possible.

Ryland lifted his head, gave her a somewhat pained grin, and lowered her back down to the bed before grabbing his weeping cock in a chokehold. "Be right back," he ground out.

Harper watched him stride a little unevenly across the room and disappear into the bathroom. Her eyes were glued to his sexy ass and she knew she was in dangerous territory.

And she wasn't talking about the men who were trying to kill them.

If she wasn't careful, Ryland Mills could easily make her fall in love with him.

******

After taking care of himself with a few, quick pumps, Ryland wandered back into the bedroom, snagged his pajama bottoms from his duffel bag and put them on. If he stayed naked, he'd be too tempted to fuck Harper. And he promised tonight would be about her. At this point, he was sort of regretting that promise—at least his poor dick was.

Ryland looked down at Harper, stretched out like a content feline, and smirked. He was the one who put that satiated look on her gorgeous face and before the night was over, he vowed to do it again.

"Move your sexy ass over," he said and crawled into the bed beside her. Pulling her close, right up against his side, he breathed her soft vanilla-coconut scent in deeply. "Fuck, you smell good." He nuzzled his face in her hair, the silky strands tickling his nose, and she snuggled against him.

"Tonight doesn't have to be just about me, you know," she murmured.

The desire to flip her over and sink into her sweet, soaking wet depths was nearly his undoing. "As tempting as that sounds, you're the one who's going to get all the orgasms tonight, sweetheart."

Lifting her blonde head and propping her chin in her palm, she studied him with those gorgeous aqua eyes. "Why?"

"Because you deserve to be worshiped." He toyed with a golden strand of her hair. It felt like silk against his rough fingertips. She was so small, delicate and feminine. The complete opposite of him, yet he had a feeling they'd fit together perfectly. In every way—physically, mentally, emotionally. He'd never had a partner before—other than his teammates—but they didn't count. Not like this.

This was all new territory, but he liked it. Harper awakened something deep inside him and he wanted to explore whatever connection they seemed to have. Their chemistry was electric and the fierce protectiveness she stirred up within him made him want to claim her. Mark her as his.

He wouldn't let anything bad happen to her. And if anyone threatened her? He'd kill them without thinking twice.

"Thank you for letting me call my sister," she said and pressed a kiss above his heart.

"You guys are really close. I didn't want her to worry."

"You're really sweet. You know that?"

Sweet? She was the only one who'd ever described him as sweet. "I don't know about that."

"How're you doing?"

Her soft question caught him by surprise and he arched a dark brow. "Me? You're the one whose entire life was just flipped upside down."

"But you lost a friend."

An image of Tanner filled his head and Ryland tried not to let his emotions surface. Keeping them locked up tight was essential in helping him focus his energy on taking down the assholes behind The Agency.

But her reminder was also a slap in the face about the reality of their situation. This wasn't a vacation in paradise. His team was in danger. She was in danger. All because of who he was. And what he did for a living.

"I loved Tanner like a brother, but I can't let myself mourn right now." He studied the innocent look in her eyes. She was gazing at him like he was some kind of hero or something. "Harper, make no mistake about who I am and what I do."

"What do you mean? You take down the bad guys, right?"

"I follow orders. I don't do background checks on my targets; I hunt them down and take them out. I'm an assassin trained by the government, not some kind of hero."

"You help keep this country safe."

"Yes, but don't look at me like that."

"Like what?"

"Like I'm the good guy."

"But you were a SEAL."

"There's only one thing I am—and that's a killer."

Ryland knew he was being blunt and maybe too direct. Cruel even. But she needed to understand he wasn't a saint. Far from it. He was an avenging angel who sought justice. And when it came to Tanner, he would dole out a fiery vengeance against the fuckers who murdered his friend as soon as the opportunity presented itself.

******

Harper knew Ryland was trying to scare her, but she wasn't frightened of who he was or what he'd done. In fact, his intentions to intimidate her were backfiring. She'd never had anyone step up to protect her like he did and it made her like him even more.

Yes, his job might require him to do difficult and unsavory things, but as she laid there in his strong arms, a couple of things struck her. First, he promised that tonight was all about her and he'd kept his word. Even though he wanted her—and she could feel the hard evidence pressed against her most of the night—he was an unselfish lover.

Because he'd kept his promise, she trusted him.

162

Harper didn't have much faith in men after the way her ex treated her, but Ryland was restoring her belief in the possibility of a happy ending. With each touch and every kind word, her self-esteem rose a notch. It had been a long time since she'd felt so good about a man and possibly pursuing something with him.

But did Ryland feel the same way? Was he interested in her long term? Or was this merely a brief dalliance until he and his team stopped The Agency? Maybe she was just a convenient distraction for him. Those thoughts were keeping her up when she should've been sleeping.

"Why're you still up?" Ryland murmured.

It was almost three in the morning and her questions about the future were making her head spin. But she couldn't tell him. God, they hadn't even had an official first date yet and here she was obsessing over the hot former SEAL in her bed who'd made her come harder than she thought possible. More than once.

If he was that talented with his mouth and fingers, she could only imagine what he could do with his—

"Harper?"

"Hmm?"

"Aren't you tired, sweetheart?"

"I can't sleep," she admitted.

163

He pulled back and eyed her in the dim room lit only by moonlight. "Do you want me to sleep in the other room? Would that make you more comfortable?"

"No!" His words made her chest tighten. Did he even realize how thoughtful he was? "Just hold me. Please."

"Always." Ryland lifted his arm and she tucked herself against his side.

Harper wasn't sure how much time they had together, but she wasn't about to waste any of it. Maybe this would all be over in a few days or a week. Despite his promise, or maybe because of it, she slid her hand down his chest, along his flat abs and straight down the front of his pajama bottoms.

"Harper," he rasped.

"You promised last night was all about me. Well, now it's well past midnight and I want you, Ryland. All of you." Her fingers wrapped around his hardening length and she stroked until his cock was standing upright, hot and throbbing in her hand.

"Are you sure?" he asked, voice strained. He grabbed her wrist, halting its movements and she lightly squeezed. "Because you're killing me right now."

"I've never been so sure of anything in my life. I want you inside me. Please."

Ryland pulled her hand out of his pants and flipped her onto her back. His mouth slammed against hers and their tongues dueled. The kiss fueled the fire burning through Harper's body and she arched up, pressing her center against him and circling her hips.

With a groan, Ryland tugged his pants off then dragged her panties and shorts down, tossing them aside. His hand moved between their bodies and when he touched her, she cried out. She'd never felt so desperate for anyone in her life, and if she didn't have Ryland soon, it felt like she was going to die.

"Shirt off," he ordered, pulling it up. "I need to see you. Taste you everywhere." She helped maneuver it over her head and they threw it aside.

Ryland pushed back onto his heels, and she shivered as his scorching gaze slid over her naked body.

"Fuck, sweetheart," he growled, drinking her in from head to toe. "You're the most beautiful thing I've ever seen." After admiring her, he lowered himself back down onto his elbows and centered his attention on her breasts.

Breathing hard, Harper let her head fall back as she savored every toe-curling sensation that shot through her body. Ryland lapped and licked and laved, sucking one taut, rosy nipple into his mouth and then the other.

"You taste like heaven." His mouth moved upward,

leaving a trail of hot kisses across her collarbone, and she moaned softly when he began sucking on her neck.

"You're going to give me a hickey," she murmured.

"Good."

"Ryland!"

He lifted his head and locked her in his sights. "You're mine, Harper, and I want everyone to know it."

The possessive tone in his voice shot an arrow of heat straight to her core. Then his fingers were on her clit and she cried out. Her entire body was overheating fast and he slid two fingers inside her. Curling...stroking...scissoring...massaging her clit until everything tightened then released in a glorious series of spasms that vibrated through her entire body.

A scream burst from Harper's mouth and Ryland smothered it, sucking her tongue into his mouth, kissing her hard and deep. When he rolled off her, she moaned at the loss of his hot skin against hers.

"Hang on." He rummaged around in his duffel bag and returned a moment later. Her passion-glazed eyes watched him tear open the packet and roll the condom on. It looked like his hands shook, but she couldn't tell for sure. Then he positioned himself between her thighs and when his engorged tip touched her leaking center, she lifted her hips, welcoming him.

"Do it, Ryland. God, *please...*" Yep, that was definitely desperation in her voice. But he held back, teasing her mercilessly, cock fisted and dragging himself up and down her dripping slit.

"Open up for me, sweetheart."

Her legs fell apart and he began to push inside. As her body expanded around his large girth, Harper cried out. The sensation of being completely full and stretched around his big, hard cock left Harper gasping.

"Okay?"

She forced a nod.

"Say the words. Tell me to keep going."

"Keep going!" She shouted the words and he laughed at her boisterous encouragement.

"Just making sure you're good," he murmured and pressed a kiss to her lips. He began to move his hips, thrusting, sliding his cock in and out. The sweet friction kept building, deeper and harder, until their bodies were slick with perspiration and moving in unison.

Although Harper wasn't a virgin, she was in new territory. With every movement, every stroke, every whispered endearment, Ryland was stripping away old insecurities and giving her a newfound confidence and freedom, something she'd always lacked in the bedroom.

And it felt amazing.

Giving herself over to sensation, offering herself to him completely, Harper willingly soared off the edge of the cliff and shattered in orgasmic bliss.

Chapter Thirteen

The moment Harper came undone, Ryland lost the little bit of control he'd managed to hang on to. His body shuddered hard above her, and he let out a long, primal groan as his release tore through him.

"Fuuuck…" He dropped down beside her with an *oomph* and it took him a moment to regroup. What in the hell just happened? Staring up at the ceiling, Ryland could only blink as he came down from the best sex he ever had. Unable to move, completely caught off guard, he enjoyed the final few spasms of pleasure that rolled through his body before slipping out of bed and getting rid of the condom.

Once he returned, he pulled Harper into his arms and pressed a kiss to her wild, blonde waves. She cuddled closer and he immediately knew he could get used to this.

Drowsiness fell over him and tropical vanilla filled his senses as he drifted off.

It felt like he'd only been asleep a couple of hours when his phone started buzzing, rousing him from the deep, comfortable sleep. The best sleep he'd had in a while. Yawning, he reached over and grabbed the phone off the nightstand, a little startled to see it was already seven a.m. The military had made him a morning person and, normally, he was up before seven. Glancing over at Harper, stretched out beside him, he knew why he'd been sleeping so soundly. It was because of her.

Everything about her felt right. No other lover had ever given him such a sense of contentment. It left him a little out of sorts and had him picturing things he usually didn't—marriage, kids, a future.

And that was dangerous territory for a guy like him who lived from mission to mission with no guarantee of returning. Plus now there was the extra added chaos of being hunted by The Agency.

Pulling his attention off her and to the reason he was awake, he opened the text from Banshee. After reading it, he bolted up, hopped out of bed and threw on a t-shirt and cargo pants. He used the bathroom quickly and returned to the bedroom just as Harper started to stir in the bed.

Her eyes fluttered open and her voice was thick with sleep. "What's going on?"

170

"Banshee decrypted part of the list."

"For The Agency?" She sat up, pulling the sheet under her arms, and Ryland took a moment to admire her cute bed head and sleepy eyes.

"Yeah. I'm going over to his bungalow now. Sleep in, if you want."

"I'll come over after I get dressed. You think there's anywhere around here to get coffee?"

"Don't worry. Bruja will already have it hot and waiting for us. She can't survive without it."

"Good to know."

Ryland paused, soaking in the blonde beauty he had gotten to know quite well last night. Her shapely calf was peeking out from beneath the sheet and the sight of her cleavage made his mouth water. In three steps, he reached the bed, dropped a knee on the mattress and leaned over. He cupped her face and kissed her, forcing himself to pull back before he lost sight of his mission and devoured her.

"Good morning," he murmured, thumbs circling her cheekbones.

She blinked sleepily several times and gave him a lazy smile. "Good morning."

"I'd love to spend the day in bed with you," he said

and dropped a kiss at the corner of her mouth, "but we've got work to do."

"Raincheck?" she asked, eyes twinkling.

"That'll be a hell yeah," he growled. He started to get up then said, "Fuckit," grabbed her face again, and kissed the shit out of her. She was irresistible and he was having a hard time leaving her.

Ryland never found it difficult to jet after sex—there was usually a trail of smoke in his wake—but he found himself lingering with Harper. With her, he wanted…more.

Finally, she broke their kiss and frowned. Covering her mouth, she said, "I have gross morning breath."

"No. You're perfect." He trailed a finger along the top of the draping sheet, skimming over the plump curve of her breast. "Last night was perfect."

Harper pressed her lips together and suddenly looked shy. *So fucking adorable.*

"I should go," Ryland murmured, trying to ignore the way her nipple hardened into a tight little bud beneath his touch. "See you shortly."

"Okay," she whispered.

Unable to help himself, he lightly squeezed her breast and kissed her again. Then he dragged himself away before he gave in and jumped her.

******

After Ryland left, Harper sighed dreamily. Last night was amazing in every way and for a few minutes, she lingered in bed, reviewing the highlight reel. His kisses, touches and naughty whispers imprinted themselves on her mind. No one had ever made her come alive like he did. He gave her the security and safety to let go of her inhibitions and doubts. He showed her what true intimacy felt like and encouraged her to give in to the passion between them.

And talk about passion. Holy hell, she'd never felt anything quite so intense. Her body was still tingling. Ryland Mills had blown her mind in every possible way and she was craving him on a primal level. Wanting to feel his big hands all over her, his mouth and tongue exploring her skin and his cock deep inside her.

"Shit," Harper whispered. After one night, she was falling for him and she had no idea where he stood. Dragging herself out of bed, she wandered into the bathroom and washed up. There was no denying the aftersex glow. Or the hickey. Consumed by thoughts of Ryland, she pulled on some of the clothes Bruja had let her borrow, drew her hair back in a low ponytail and headed over to Banshee and Bruja's bungalow.

The crew was gathered together in the living room area and the moment she walked in the door, Ryland came over to meet her. She could feel all eyes on them as he dropped a quick kiss on her lips. Apparently, he had no problem with letting his team know—

Know what? That they were sleeping together? An item now? She had no idea what they were exactly and her cheeks heated up as he threaded his fingers through hers and led her over to the group.

One thing was certain, though. He'd claimed her as his and he was letting them all know it.

Ryland tugged Harper down on the couch beside him and she glanced up at Bruja who came over, grinning broadly, and handed her a mug of steaming coffee.

"Heard you need some caffeine." She winked and Harper mumbled a thanks, feeling the blush creep down her neck. She brought the mug up to inhale the brewed goodness, using it as a cover to avoid everyone else's eyes.

"Okay," Pharaoh said, getting down to business. "Banshee has a list of ten names and he's managed to decrypt two."

"Targets?" Ryland asked.

"The first target is Lester Tillman. According to my search, he lives in the San Diego area. Comes from money and never worked a day in his life. I wouldn't be surprised if he's helping to bankroll The Agency. Target two is Selma Santiago. Haven't found much on her yet, but it looks like she has a residence located a couple of hours away in Ensenada."

"What's the plan?" Saint asked. "My Spanish is *muy mal* so I'd rather deal with Tillman."

"Santiago doesn't necessarily mean Spanish, Saint." Bruja rolled her eyes.

Pharaoh nodded. "Bruja and Rip, track down Santiago. Recon only. Saint and I will head back to San Diego and see if we can find Tillman, and Banshee will be our eyes and ears here at command center."

"Recon only?" Ryland echoed through gritted teeth.

Beside her, his body tensed and there was no missing the disapproval in his tone.

"Recon only," Pharaoh stated firmly. Then his tone softened. "Don't worry, Rip. We'll get the fuckers who took out Tanner. But we can't go running around, half-cocked, shooting shit up. We need to make sure and the last thing we want to do is tip them off before we understand fully who all we're dealing with."

Ryland forced a nod and Harper felt the frustration vibrating through him. But she had to agree with Pharaoh. They needed to clearly identify their targets and the bad people within The Agency first.

"Then let's pay Selma Santiago a visit because I've

got a lot of fucking questions about what's going on." Ryland stood up, ready to go.

"Stay in touch and lock it down," Pharaoh ordered, squeezing Ryland's shoulder. "We'll reconvene tonight."

With a sharp nod, Ryland walked out and Harper stood up, ready to follow him. She wasn't exactly sure what her part in all of this would be, but she knew Ryland wouldn't leave her behind.

Apparently, she wasn't the only one who figured that out. After watching Ryland stalk away, Pharaoh turned his intense attention to her. "Can you keep him in line?" He looked from Harper to Bruja. "Because we can't afford for him to lose it."

"We can handle him," Bruja assured him and exchanged a look with Harper.

Could she handle him? Harper wasn't exactly sure, but she nodded anyway. She already knew she would do her best to ensure The Agency was made to pay for their crimes against Ryland and his team. And she'd be right beside him, ready to talk him down if he escalated.

"C'mon, Harper. Let's go."

With no idea what to expect, Harper pulled in a deep breath and followed Bruja.

******

176

Ryland drove his father's Ford Explorer while Pharaoh and Saint took the Suburban and headed back north. Leaving Banshee at the bungalow, they settled in for the two-hour drive. Harper sat in the passenger seat and he could feel her gaze on him, but he kept his attention on the dirt road.

He had a lot of questions for Santiago and if she didn't cooperate, there would be a serious problem. The anger and pain he'd tamped down and compartmentalized over Tanner's death was seeping through, like a battery leaking acid, and he itched to take it out on someone.

If he found out she was the asshole behind Tanner's death, he wouldn't hesitate to pull the trigger. Fuck recon.

Stewing in his dark thoughts, he barely noticed when Harper's hand slid over his and squeezed.

"Hey," she murmured, her soft voice cutting through his angry haze. "Come back to me."

Ryland glanced over at her. She was all light and goodness, a pure soul, and he hated himself for dragging her into this tangled web. But here she was and there was nothing he could do about it. Nothing except protect her and keep her out of harm's way.

They reached their destination and Ryland double-checked the address before parking the Explorer down the street and out of sight. Selma Santiago lived in Greater Ensenada which was outside the main area of the city and more of a coastal beach town. It had several renowned surfing spots and Ryland paused, his attention going straight to the Pacific Ocean to check out the wave height. He knew Todos Santos Island was located about two hours off the coastline and where the Billabong XXL surfing contest was held. Wave faces could reach sixty feet out there, and he and Tanner had talked about going one day.

Now that would never happen.

Gritting his teeth, Ryland communicated to Bruja with a hand gesture, motioning for her to circle around to the back of the house while he and Harper would stay in the front.

Bruja nodded and disappeared into the yard.

"Are you ready to put your acting skills to work?" Ryland asked, grabbing Harper's hand.

"I'm not a very good actor," Harper said, her face falling slightly.

"I'll take the lead. You just look at me with stars in your eyes."

"I think I can do that."

Ryland smirked, lifted his hand and knocked on the door. "That's right, Mrs. Mills. We just got married and now we're down here on our honeymoon. Too bad our car just broke down."

The corner of her mouth lifted in a knowing grin.

Mrs. Mills. Ryland never gave much thought about there being a missus, but when he looked at Harper, he began giving it some serious consideration. Or maybe the sun was too hot down here and he was losing his mind.

He was about to knock again when the door opened and a dark-haired woman who looked to be somewhere in her forties arched a thin brow. She had a haughty air to her and before she could say a word, Ryland launched into his bullshit story.

"We're so sorry to bother you, *señorita*, but my wife and I are on our honeymoon. We're having some car trouble and wonder if we can use your phone?" Ryland gave her a lopsided grin when she didn't say anything. "I sure hope you *habla inglés*."

Her dark brown eyes narrowed. "I'm sorry, I don't have a landline," she responded in flawless, lightly-accented English. But the snotty tone in her voice told him she wasn't sorry at all. In fact, she didn't give a rat's ass. Ryland had always been able to read people and situations well, and this woman was a cold one.

"What about a cell phone? Just real quick and then we'll be on our way."

"No, I can't help you." When she began to close the door, Ryland jammed his foot in, stopping it.

"I think you can help us, Ms. Santiago," he murmured in a low, lethal voice. "Now I suggest you invite us in because we have some questions for you. And you probably wouldn't want your neighbors to overhear them."

Chapter Fourteen

Selma Santiago's dark eyes widened and before she could respond, Ryland shoved the door open, pulling Harper in behind him.

"You need to leave. Right now!" she exclaimed.

"We're not going anywhere," Bruja stated, moving up behind her. "Not until you answer our questions. *Lo entiendes?*"

"Who are you?" Selma sputtered, backing away.

"Sit," Ryland ordered, nodding to the pristine white couch. He lifted his t-shirt just enough for her to see the gun holstered at his side. "Is anyone else home?"

Reluctantly, Selma took a seat. "Not at present."

"I take it you don't recognize me or her," Ryland

said, motioning between him and Bruja.

"Should I? I think you have the wrong house."

"Does the name Ex Nihilo ring any bells?" Ryland asked, studying her closely.

No one missed the recognition that briefly flared in her guarded eyes.

"I have no idea what you're talking about," she insisted.

"Think hard," Bruja said. "We know you're a part of The Agency."

For a moment, Ryland thought she was going to deny it, but then her shoulders sank and resignation filled her face. "I didn't want to be. But my husband forced my involvement."

"Why would he force you?" Bruja asked.

"Because he's a power-hungry bastard and knew we'd have more control if we both sat at the table."

"What's your husband's name?" Ryland asked.

"Marcus Santiago." Her gaze flitted from Ryland to Bruja to Harper, as though she were trying to decide who, if any of them, she could trust. "He's a horrible man. He doesn't know it yet, but I'm in the process of filing for a divorce."

Ryland made a mental note. *Name number three: Marcus Santiago.*

Her attention landed back on Harper and she began to wring her hands, talking directly to her. Ryland got the instant impression she'd quickly identified her as the weak link and was playing on Harper's sympathy.

"He threatens me all the time and, if I don't do exactly as he says, he beats me. I have no choice." She turned her arm to show a bruise. Of course, she could've gotten that anywhere and Ryland wasn't buying what Selma was selling.

"And he forced you to be a part of The Agency?" Harper asked softly.

"That's right."

"I'm so sorry. I know what it's like to be pressured into doing things you don't want to do in order to please people you care about."

Ryland suppressed a smirk when he realized Harper was a much better actor than she'd given herself credit for. He could tell she was fishing for intel and, by playing the naive blonde, she was making Selma feel like the one in power.

Clever girl. She was playing it up like a pro and Ryland was more than a little impressed, and so damn proud of her, watching as she smoothly took control of the interrogation without making Selma withdraw or shut down.

Not a good actor? Who had put that bullshit in her head? Hell, he was half-convinced himself.

"I got sucked into the whole thing without any say. The only thing I can do now is leave him."

"Because you're scared your husband will hurt you," Harper said.

"Yes, that's right." She turned her attention to Ryland. "Are you a part of Ex Nihilo?"

"I'm asking the questions here. And I want to know why the hell my team was fucked over in Abu Dhabi. Who made the call to take us out and why?"

For a moment, Selma didn't respond and Ryland knew it was because she was mentally crafting her story. "It was determined your team can't be trusted," she finally said.

"Why not?" he prodded.

Selma looked him straight in the eye. "Because one or more of you is a traitor."

Stunned silence filled the room.

"What? That's ridiculous," Bruja commented.

"It's bullshit," Ryland agreed.

Selma tilted her chin up. "Really? Then how is information leaking?"

"What're you talking about?" Ryland demanded. "What information?"

"After your mission in South America, intel from that op was leaked. As a result, part of the cartel your team helped bring down escaped. It was deduced that someone from Ex Nihilo warned the cartel members. That someone is playing both sides."

"No," Ryland said. "Didn't happen."

"Tell me," Selma said, voice silky. "How well do you know the people you work with?"

Her question lingered in the air and Ryland felt the hair on the back of his neck stand up. He resisted the urge to reach around and rub the skin there.

"If I'm not mistaken, your team was only put together six months ago and you don't even know each other's real names. You came together as strangers, right?"

"We're a cohesive unit that trusts each other with our lives," Bruja said, bristling.

"Maybe that's not so wise." Selma glanced down at her manicured nails then waved a hand. "Anyway, that's all I know."

Yeah, right. "We want a list of names. All ten people that make up The Agency."

One of her thin, dark eyebrows arched. "I don't know anyone's real name. Other than my husband's, of course. Same as you and your team. If you'd like to question Marcus, then by all means, go ahead. I can assure you, he knows more than me, but he won't be back until later. Would you like anything to drink while you wait? He should be home in a couple of hours."

Selma Santiago was one smooth customer and Ryland had a hard time believing anything that came out of her over-inflated, red lips. The only thing that remotely rang true was The Agency following the same protocol as Ryland's team and only using aliases. He and Tanner had broken the rules, became friends and gotten buddy-buddy. But the others were still just Pharaoh, Saint, Banshee and Bruja.

He glared at Selma then glanced over at Bruja who crossed her arms. She didn't appear to be buying the woman's bullshit either.

Placing her well-manicured hands on her thighs, Santiago moved her gaze between the three of them and stood. "Well, if you'll excuse me, I'm going to get myself a mineral water. It's far too hot today."

"Actually, that sounds good. Why don't I go with you?" Bruja stood up and Ryland watched them start walking away.

Halfway out of the living room, Selma paused and turned. "I'm sorry to be the one to tell you there's a mole on your team. But think back on your missions and try to remember the way your teammates acted. What they said and did. You may be able to figure out who the double agent is yourself. But, in the meantime, The Agency doesn't trust any of you. That's why you're on their kill list. And once you become their target, there's no escaping. They will hunt each one of your team down and eliminate you all."

Turning on her heel, Selma walked out, Bruja directly behind her. Her ominous words rankled Ryland and he wanted to brush them off. But something inside of him couldn't help but wonder if there was any truth to her claims.

A double agent? He had a hard time believing it, but he also wasn't stupid enough to completely toss the theory out the window. She had a point about Ex Nihilo. Though they worked well together, they didn't know each other like he'd known his former SEAL team. Hell, he didn't even know anyone's true name.

Yes, they worked seamlessly as a unit. But could he trust them? *Shit.*

Ryland scraped a hand over his jaw and met Harper's steady gaze. "She's trying to plant seeds of doubt," Harper said. "You trust your team. Right?"

Normally, he'd say yes. But the more he thought

about it, how well did he really know any of them?

He fucking didn't.

"Ryland?"

"Christ, Harper, I can't talk about this right now."

She closed her mouth and he tried to tamp down the uncertainty and suspicions suddenly flooding his brain.

A loud, pained shout made his head snap up and he jumped to his feet, running straight to the kitchen. Bruja was lying on the floor, her entire body twitching.

Harper dropped down beside Bruja. "What's wrong with her?"

"Taser," Ryland answered between gritted teeth. "She'll be okay."

He stomped over to the open back door where Selma most likely fled. He stepped outside onto the back patio and pulled his gun, gaze searching the expanse of empty beach. "Where the hell are you?"

Stepping off the edge of the deck, he circled the house, reaching the front just as a sporty, red convertible shot out of the garage and roared headlong into the street.

Seething, head full of doubts, Ryland watched Selma Santiago make her escape.

And he was more confused than ever.

******

The ride back was tense and Harper could feel the change in Ryland. That sneaky bitch. Selma had managed to rock his faith in the very people he should trust the most. Granted, Harper didn't know Ryland's team very well, but what she saw told her they were a good group of people.

She wished she'd been able to meet Tanner. Losing him had hurt Ryland immensely—she could see it in his eyes every time his friend's name came up.

By the time they arrived at the bungalows, Pharaoh and Saint had already returned. They informed the others that Tillman was MIA and they had no more information on him. Meanwhile, Ryland and Bruja filled them in on the conversation with Selma Santiago and how she'd revealed her husband was also a part of The Agency. Then how she'd run off after tasing Bruja.

"That *puta* had it hidden in the drawer. By the time I realized it, she'd hit the trigger."

"You think she's hiding something?" Pharaoh asked.

"Definitely," Ryland said. "Why else would she run?"

"Maybe she went to warn her husband," Saint offered.

Or maybe she was lying about everything, Harper thought. She hardly seemed like a trustworthy person.

"I'm going to run searches on Marcus Santiago and see what else I can dig up on Tillman," Banshee said. "Hang tight."

"I'm starving," Bruja announced. "Nothing like fifty thousand volts to send your metabolism into high gear. Harper, you want to help me throw some food together?"

"Sure." Harper looked over at Ryland who nodded.

"Just no mango, okay?" he joked.

"No mango," she agreed, and Banshee made a scoffing sound.

The women moved into the kitchen and started chopping up the fresh fruit Banshee had brought in earlier. The more time she spent with Bruja, the more Harper liked her. But she held her cards close to her chest like the rest of his team. She knew they'd been ordered to, but it sure made it harder to get to know them better.

"You mentioned you were in the Army?" Harper asked.

"That's right," Bruja stated, slicing up a pineapple.

"What made you choose a military career?"

For a moment, she thought the other woman wasn't

going to answer. But then she said, "I'm a military brat. It's all I ever knew." She gave a shrug and dumped the pineapple chunks into a bowl.

"Did you like it?"

"I like how it challenged me. Of course, it's never easy being a woman in a male-dominated world and the military can be filled with a lot of testosterone. So I learned to be tough and not take anyone's shit. And, somehow, I managed to maintain my femininity."

"It must be hard being on a team of just men."

"I prefer it, actually. Women can get catty and hold grudges while men might argue or get in a pissing contest but, at the end of the day, you have to trust your team. And, in my experience, men work out their differences more quickly and easily than women." Her face darkened and Harper had a feeling there was more to her story.

"Well, I admire you and can't help but be a little jealous," Harper admitted as she peeled an orange.

"Jealous? Of me?" Bruja asked, her voice laced in amazement. Then she let out a self-deprecating chuckle. "Don't be. Besides, you're the gorgeous blonde sporting a hickey, Harper. Not me."

Her face reddened and Harper immediately reached up and laid a hand on her neck. Right over the spot where Ryland had sucked and kissed hard enough to leave a mark. Her blood instantly heated at the memory. "Oh, God," she mumbled. "Do you think everyone noticed?"

"Pretty sure," Bruja announced cheerfully.

"I'm so embarrassed."

"Don't be. Ryland really likes you and I get the feeling you're going to be good for him. Especially after losing Mayhem. Everyone knew how close they'd gotten and even though he's shutting his grief down, make no mistake about it—he's hurting. Badly. And his asshole father isn't helping matters."

Harper knew the other woman was right. "I'm going to do everything I can to help him."

"Good."

Setting the bowl of fruit aside, Harper tilted her head and studied Bruja. She felt silly calling her by the nickname, especially since she wasn't a part of their team. "Can I ask you a question? What's your real—"

There was a sudden whoop from the other room and the women turned. "What's going on?" Bruja asked, wiping her hands off.

"We got a lead on Tillman," Pharaoh announced just as the door opened, and Cross walked into the bungalow.

"Tillman is on vacation in the Caribbean," Ryland

said. "At a couples' resort."

"So now what?" Bruja asked, hand on her hip.

"We're going in undercover," Ryland announced, looking at Harper.

"We?" Harper echoed.

"Yeah, you and me. Is that okay? I could take Bruja, but there's a bit of a catch."

The rest of the team exchanged smirks.

"What kind of catch?" Harper asked.

"It's a swingers club."

Chapter Fifteen

"Yeah, you can take your girlfriend," Bruja said. "I'd rather not be naked and have sex with a bunch of strangers. Or you for that matter."

Harper's aqua eyes widened comically and Ryland decided she was hands-down the most adorable fucking thing he'd ever seen.

"Gee, thanks, Bruja. My ego and I appreciate it," he replied dryly then turned his attention fully on Harper. "You're not going to have sex with any strangers. Me? Yeah, definitely. But no one else. So don't worry, sweetheart."

"No one's having sex," Pharaoh clipped. "This isn't a vacation. You're going in undercover and breaking into Lester Tillman's room. You'll find his laptop, use Banshee's gadget to copy everything on there and upload it to him. Then you return back here."

"Lighten up, Pharaoh," Banshee said. "At least let our man have a quickie on the beach."

"You're wound too tight. We need to get you laid," Saint teased and punched Pharaoh's arm.

Pharaoh rolled his eyes. "Thanks for the concern, but I don't need your help in that department."

"Your hand doesn't count, bro," Ryland said, and everyone laughed. Except Cross who cleared his throat and looked uncomfortable. "Don't worry, we'll get the job done. Question is, how are we getting to Jamaica?"

"I can hook you up with a private flight," Cross answered. "I have a contact in Rosarito who can be fueled and ready to go tonight."

"I'm going to need both your pictures and I'll set up some fake passports and IDs," Banshee said. "Won't take me long."

"Go pack your bags," Pharaoh announced and glanced down at his large watch, all business. "You'll leave within the hour."

"Not that you'll need many clothes," Saint commented with a chuckle.

"What do you mean?" Harper asked, tilting her blonde head.

"It's not just a swingers club. It's a nudist resort." Saint slapped Ryland between his shoulders and Harper's jaw dropped. "Have fun."

******

Exactly one hour later, Ryland and Harper arrived in Rosarito and climbed aboard the small aircraft waiting on the private landing strip. There wasn't a lot of room to maneuver around like in the jet that his team normally took, but it would get them to Jamaica sooner rather than later.

The flight should take less than six hours which had them arriving in Negril at almost three in the morning. The plan was to head to the resort, check in and sleep for a few hours. Then when morning came, they would search for Lester Tillman and his partner.

"Banshee thinks he's so funny," Ryland grumbled, looking down at the fake passport in his hand. "Fred Rogers? Really? He takes things too literally."

Harper couldn't help but chuckle and she sang softly, "It's a beautiful day in this neighborhood, a beautiful day for a neighbor, would you be mine? Could you be mine?"

Yep. So damn adorable. Ryland caught her chin in his hand and pressed a kiss to her lips, silencing the song. After a moment, he pulled away, brushed a blonde lock behind her ear and said, "I'll be all yours, neighbor."

Harper smiled and he nodded at the passport in her hand.

"Please tell me he didn't make you Ginger."

"No," she said and laughed. "I'm Annabelle Rogers. I kind of like it. Do you think I look like an Annabelle?"

"I think you look like a Harper," he said and tickled her side. "What's your middle name?"

Harper squealed, pulling away. "Lane. What's yours?"

"Harper Lane. I really like that." He cleared his throat, not wanting to talk about how he shared a middle name with a lowlife thief.

But she asked again. "Ryland what?"

He made a face. "Ryland Vincenzo Mills. Stupid, I know."

Her brows lifted, clearly not expecting that zinger. "Is it a family name?"

"Yeah, something like that."

"Why're you being so cagey?"

"Am I?"

"Answering a question with a question?"

"How about a kiss with a kiss?" He slanted his

mouth down over hers and drank deeply, putting an end to their conversation about middle names.

Once they broke apart, Harper turned serious. "So what should I know about this place?"

Ryland heard the uneasiness in her voice and reached over to cover her leg with his hand. "You mean you don't usually visit swingers resorts?" he teased and lightly squeezed.

"Um, no. Do you?"

"Never been and never planned to go. But here we are." He couldn't deny he was looking forward to going to Desire with Harper. The hotel's reputation was legendary.

"Just so you know, I'm not leaving the room if we have to be naked."

A bark of laughter burst from Ryland's throat. "They aren't nudists, sweetheart. Saint's an idiot. You're allowed to wear clothes."

"So, then what? People just have sex with other people?"

"If they want," he said carefully. "Banshee did some research on the place and said they promote it as a place for like-minded couples to explore some of their deepest desires in a safe, judgment-free zone." He shrugged a shoulder. "He also said there's live entertainment, themed parties, snorkeling and sex spots."

"Sex spots?" she echoed, wrinkling her nose.

"Don't worry. We won't be participating." His cobalt eyes dragged down her body and back up. "I don't share."

"Same." The corner of her mouth edged up. "And if anyone tries anything with you, I may resort to scratching their eyes out."

"Fine by me." He leaned in and captured her mouth in a long, lingering kiss. One that seared him, stirring something too deep to consider at that moment. Taking his time, he explored her lips and mouth thoroughly, and stifled a groan. God, she tasted sweeter than the pineapple they'd eaten earlier. Finally, he broke the kiss, pulled in a breath and said, "Although I wouldn't be opposed to having some fun with just you after we find Tillman."

"That could be arranged," she said saucily. "Just no trading partners."

Ryland caught her bottom lip between his teeth, gently nibbling there for a moment, then stroked his tongue along the seam. "You should rest. It's a long flight."

He wrapped an arm around her shoulders, encouraging her to lay her head against him. It didn't take long for her to drift off and he listened to her steady breathing.

Trade partners? Was she insane?

"Not in a million years, not for a million dollars," he murmured against her silky hair.

The rest of the flight went smoothly and after landing in Negril, they lucked out and caught a lone taxi to drive them to Desire.

After paying the driver, Ryland lifted both their bags from the trunk and hoisted them over his shoulder. Check-in was quick and the desk attendant was miraculously awake at that hour. Afterwards, they found their room easily.

"Oh, my God," Harper murmured, looking around the suite and sliding open the back door. "This place is fantastic. Ryland, there's a private hot tub out here!"

Suppressing a grin, Ryland walked over where Harper was oohing and ahhing over the jacuzzi like she'd never seen one before. He moved up behind her, wrapping his arms around her waist, and pressed a kiss to her neck. "Hopefully, we'll have time to try it. But right now, we need some sleep. Tomorrow is going to be a long day, Mrs. Rogers."

The back story they came up with for Fred and Annabelle Rogers was pretty simple: they've been married a few years and growing a little bored with their current, vanilla lifestyle. They heard about the swingers resort from a friend and were always curious, so they decided to check it out.

For a moment, Ryland imagined what it would be like marrying this woman and how their lives would look a few years later. He couldn't imagine wanting anyone else other than this exciting woman who made his pulse quicken.

With a soft sigh, Harper leaned back in his arms and he scooped her up, carried her inside and laid her on the huge king-size bed. The temptation to strip her bare and spend the rest of the night playing with that luscious body of hers was nearly overwhelming. But he had a mission to accomplish first and foremost.

Then, they could play.

******

Morning came fast and Ryland and Harper were up bright and early, ready to find Lester Tillman and get the job done. As much as she'd wanted to frolic in the hot tub with Ryland, she was glad they went straight to bed because she fell asleep the moment her head hit the pillow. And, if all went well, they would have plenty of time to luxuriate in their suite, and each other, before they had to head back to meet the team.

They'd decided to go down to the pool first and

scope it out. Harper had bought them bathing suits earlier down in the gift shop, as well as some more clothes for herself, and she turned in front of the bathroom mirror, doubt creeping in at her decision. It was way skimpier than she would normally wear, but the tiny two piece had been the most modest suit in the shop. She supposed since guests were allowed to strut around in their birthday suits, she probably would be wearing more than most. It was still a little out of her comfort zone and she adjusted the small piece of fabric that was supposed to be covering her bum.

It didn't seem to be doing a very good job.

She gave up trying to cover her rear and slipped the mesh coverup she'd bought over her head. At least she wasn't stuck wearing a Speedo like poor Ryland. Remembering the too-small bottoms made her snicker softly. But he had the body for it and she was looking forward to seeing how nicely he, ahem, filled it.

"Here goes nothing," she whispered to her reflection and strode out.

Ryland turned and his gaze heated up like an inferno as it skimmed down her body. Her insides melted as he reached her in two long strides, his arms wrapping around her and pulling her against his body.

"You look so damn beautiful," he murmured, pushing her blonde waves back and dropping kisses along the side of her face. When he finally found her lips, he kissed her passionately and her knees went weak.

No one had ever made her feel as desired as Ryland and she clung to the feeling, ready to explore things with him further.

"We're supposed to be bored with each other, Mr. Rogers," she reminded him. "You don't feel, ah, bored." There was no missing the way his cock was getting hard against her belly. That Speedo hid very little.

"I'm bored stiff, sweetheart," he rasped. "Every time I touch you, I feel like I'm going to explode."

"Well, you better put on a good show out there."

Ryland pulled back and groaned. "I'd give anything to stay in here all day and fuck you on every surface. In every position. Until you're nothing but a shaking, trembling mess, coming undone again and again."

A shiver ran through Harper. "Hold that thought for later," she murmured and ran her hands through the long, sun-bleached hair on top of his head.

"Alright, let's go find this asshole and hack his laptop," Ryland grunted in an annoyed voice and stepped away from her, readjusting himself with a curse. "My need for you is becoming too much to ignore."

His need for her…

She'd finally found a man who said he needed her

and looked at her with a fierce longing that turned her insides to molten lava and, of course, as her luck would dictate, some mysterious group wanted him dead.

Well, screw that. She wasn't about to let anyone take away the best thing that ever happened to her. She had plans for them and no one was going to steal away their future happiness.

******

The massive pool area was exactly what he expected from a resort promoting a hedonistic lifestyle. It was decadent and full of pleasurable things, and Ryland took everything in, scanning over the waterfalls and hidden grottos, bars featuring endless tropical drinks, blooming flowers and ferns everywhere and, of course, the guests themselves, some of whom wore nothing at all.

As they wound their way past sunbathing guests on lounge chairs, Ryland felt a lot of interested eyes on them. He wasn't surprised. Harper looked stunning in her barely-there bikini, and even though she was covered up, the mesh shirt teased enough. Hell, he'd had to wrangle his own hard-on into submission before they came out because the damn Speedo didn't hide anything.

Ryland lived half his life in board shorts, so he felt a bit confined and exposed all at the same time. *Whatever.* He surfed like a fiend, worked out and his job kept him in great physical shape. He'd rather have eyes on him than Harper because the more they ogled her, the more possessive he felt himself getting.

Breathe, Mills. He had to remind himself he was supposed to be there to swap partners and share. Which was insane. He would never share Harper with anyone. She belonged to him whether she knew it or not. As long as no one laid a hand on her, he would keep his cool.

The resort was big on kinky stuff, but also consent, so he wasn't too worried. The only one Harper would be consenting with was him. He glanced over at her and that smattering of freckles across her nose was multiplying before his very eyes from the strong sun. But that just meant all the more to kiss later on.

As they walked through the pool area, Ryland studied everyone closely from behind his sunglasses, but he didn't see Lester Tillman. The pool was a popular area and he was hoping they'd get lucky, but the man could be anywhere. The resort was huge and, for all they knew, he could still be in his room, sleeping off an eventful night of drinking and debauchery.

They found a couple of empty lounge chairs and while Ryland got comfortable, Harper pulled her coverup off and tossed it on her chair. He drew in a sharp breath. *Christ.* Swallowing hard, his unruly dick surged as she bent over and started digging through her bag.

"Sweetheart, please stand up," he begged, voice pained.

"What's wrong?" She turned and looked at him over her shoulder.

"That perfect ass of yours is going to be my undoing."

"Oh!" Harper popped up, straightening with a smirk, and lifted her bottle of sunblock. "Would you mind?"

With a low grunt, Ryland sat up and made room for her to sit on his chair. "Are you trying to kill me?" He squeezed some lotion in his hand and began rubbing it on her back and shoulders. She smelled like vanilla and coconuts, and he couldn't help himself. He leaned in and pressed a lingering kiss to the back of her neck.

"People are watching," she murmured.

"Then let's give them a show. Gotta please the voyeurs." He turned her face, tilted it up and plunged his tongue into her mouth, drinking deeply.

Chapter Sixteen

Just like she always did when he kissed her, Harper melted. He was demanding and thorough, yet she also knew he could switch it up and be incredibly tender. The man was still half a mystery to her, but Harper loved unraveling his layers as she got to know him better.

When they finally came up for air, he started dropping kisses on her nose and she laughed. "What're you doing?"

"Kissing…your…freckles," he told her, punctuating each word with another kiss.

"Oh, geez, I probably have a ton more from the sun," she lamented.

"I love them."

Love…Her stomach flipped, and she wondered what

it would be like to hear him say he loved her. *Cart before the horse,* she scolded herself. If anything, she'd be the fool who would tell him first and make things awkward.

Ryland finished kissing her nose then sat back and pulled her tight between his legs. His arms wrapped around her and he clasped his hands together, laying them against her flat stomach. It seemed like he was sending out a clear message that could very easily be interpreted as "she's mine."

"Are you trying to scare off potential partners?" Harper chuckled and he tightened his grip.

"Fuck yeah, I am."

"Any sign of Tillman?" she asked under her breath.

"Not yet," Ryland reported.

They cuddled for a while, soaking up the sun and people-watching. Harper had never seen people so free with their bodies. Some wore bathing suits, some didn't bother, but no one seemed to mind either way.

After a while, they noticed couples partnering up and disappearing either into the grotto or a large striped tent at the other end of the pool. Harper knew they'd eventually have to witness some of the sexy shenanigans going on at the resort and it looked like the time had arrived.

"Care to check out the grotto, Mrs. Rogers?"

Ryland asked in a low voice, lips brushing the shell of her ear.

Harper pulled in a nervous breath and nodded. "Sure."

Time to get into let's-swap-partners mode. Not that she would, though. Ryland was one-hundred percent her man and she wasn't interested in anyone else. She had a feeling this trip was going to really test her limited acting skills. Feigning interest in someone else just might be a role too difficult to play.

As they strolled over to the grotto and walked into the large cave-like structure behind the waterfall, Harper chewed nervously on her lower lip. The place was clearly a popular sex spot. The first thing she saw was a man and woman fucking up against the smooth wall. A few people watched them while others engaged in some seriously hot and heavy petting in groups of various sizes.

Her steps faltered and Ryland took her hand and squeezed it. When she looked up into his bright blue eyes, he whispered, "I got you."

Harper trusted him as he led her over to a dim corner and down into the warm, swirling water of a heated pool that could easily accommodate ten people. The bubbles felt amazing and she tried not to stare at the other couples who were kissing and fondling each other. Trying her best not to look uncomfortable, she followed Ryland across the pool to sit near the only couple not engaging in some form of sexual activity. When she took a closer look, she almost gasped as she recognized the man whose picture Banshee had provided.

It was Lester Tillman.

She quickly schooled her features to hide her shock at their good luck in finding him so quickly. Her discomfort took a backseat to her desire to help Ryland and his team. It was go-time. Time to get to work and find out his room number so they could break in and copy all the info on his laptop. But first, they were going to have to get buddy-buddy with him and his partner. Not something she was looking forward to doing, but that's why they were there. It was a good reminder they were not, in fact, a normal couple on vacation.

She noticed the woman's tropical drink garnished with a pineapple wedge and leaned closer. "That looks delicious," Harper said with a friendly smile. "What is it?"

"A Bahama Mama," she answered and took a sip.

"I'll have to get one of those. My husband loves pineapples," Harper added.

Tillman chuckled. "I'll bet he does. You know what they say about drinking pineapple juice."

Actually, she didn't. A slight frown drew her brows together and Ryland's mouth edged up.

"I think it works both ways," Ryland said, his hand covering her leg beneath the water.

"From my experience, drinking a good-sized glass of pineapple juice a couple of hours before the deed can help make certain bodily fluids even more enjoyable." Tillman couldn't seem to pry his eyes off Harper and she tried not to squirm.

"Is that so?" she asked, doing her best to sound at ease and sexy. "Well, then let's order a round of Bahama Mamas!"

Tillman barked out a laugh and she felt Ryland's fingers tighten around her thigh. *Sorry, Ryland, but we have to play their game.*

"I'm Annabelle and this is my husband Freddy," Harper said, doing her best to keep a straight face when she introduced Ryland.

"It's so nice to meet you, Annabelle." Tillman's eyes dipped, trying to see beneath the jacuzzi's bubbles. "I'm John and this is Jackie."

Sure, Harper thought, but she grinned, and they all shook hands. Tillman held hers for a moment too long and Ryland bristled beside her. The good news was they'd made contact and they had their first names, so now Banshee would be able to figure out what room they were staying in. The bad news was she worried Ryland would go all caveman on Tillman if he got too friendly

211

and blow their cover. But he was a trained operative, right? He'd get himself together. She placed her hand on his knee and started drawing little circles and hearts along his skin, hoping to settle his mind with a reminder that she was all his.

It wasn't hard to charm the older couple. They enjoyed the attention and Harper pulled out all the stops, flirting outrageously with them for the next forty-five minutes. Ryland did his fair share, too, and it didn't take long until Tillman was enamored with Harper and Jackie was panting over Ryland.

"Look, we have a scuba lesson in ten minutes," Tillman said, voice laced in disappointment. "But I think we'd both like to see you later."

"Definitely," Jackie added, batting her faux lashes at Ryland.

"Why don't you join us for dinner at the restaurant? Say six o'clock?" Tillman couldn't pry his eyes off Harper and she did her best to appear interested.

"Sounds like a plan," Ryland said.

"Good. We'll see you then."

Harper watched them stand up and said a silent prayer of thanks that Tillman wasn't naked. As they passed by, he reached over and trailed his fingers beneath Harper's jaw. "See you soon, Annabelle."

Holding steady, trying not to pull away from his touch, Harper forced herself to smile up at him. Beneath the bubbling water, Ryland's fingers dug into her upper thigh. "Not soon enough," she said and winked.

As they walked away, Ryland let out an annoyed sound—half frustrated sigh, half disgusted snort. "I fucking hate him," he growled.

"He's a creep. No doubt about it."

"I need to let Banshee know the first names they're going by and he should be able to get us a room number. I'll sneak in during their scuba lesson, copy the laptop and then we're out of here."

Harper nodded, relieved they wouldn't have to actually meet Tillman for dinner.

Relief that was entirely too short-lived.

******

Ryland and Harper returned to their room, changed out of their bathing suits—thank you Baby Jesus—and waited for Banshee to call with Tillman's room number. Ryland figured the couple would be occupied with snorkeling for at least an hour or two, so the timing would be perfect.

When his phone rang, Ryland snatched it up, beyond impatient to get the job done. "Banshee, tell me something good."

213

"Hey, Rip. I've got good news and bad news."

"Bad first."

"There are no guests registered under John and Jackie."

Ryland clenched his jaw. *Fucking wonderful.* Harper was looking at him expectantly and he gave a slight shake of his head. "Okay, so they're using another alias. What's the good news?"

"You get to hang out with Tillman again. Maybe this time he can borrow your Speedo."

Banshee laughed and Ryland grumbled a curse then hung up on him. Grabbing the back of his neck, he sighed. "Looks like we're going to have to meet them for dinner."

"It's okay. We have a job to do. And we need to eat, right?"

Damn, she was a trooper. "I was hoping to be long gone by then. Sorry, sweetheart. But, hey, it's just another chance for you to put those amazing acting skills of yours to use."

"Please, don't say that." Her usual sunny disposition clouded over.

"What's wrong?" he asked, frowning.

"I tried acting when I lived in L.A. and was

214

repeatedly reminded that I wasn't good enough."

"Fuck L.A.," Ryland said, immediately hating the city for making her doubt herself. "What the hell do they know?"

Her mouth edged up. "Well, it is the entertainment capital of the world, so I figured they knew something."

"They don't know shit." He locked gazes with her aqua eyes, hating the vulnerability swimming in their depths. "I believe in you."

"Thank you," she whispered.

"I do," he repeated with conviction. "You handled Santiago like a pro and I know you'll do the same with Tillman. You've already got him eating out of the palm of your hand from your performance in the jacuzzi. If I could give you an Oscar myself, I would."

She chuckled. "Forget about a gold statue. But I'm willing to bet you can make it up to me in other ways, Mr. Rogers."

Her suggestive tone made his pulse leap. "Oh, you can count on it." Ryland slid his arms around her waist.

"So, what's the plan?"

"Back to basics," he said, and she arched a brow. "You're going to distract him and be your charming self and I'm going to steal his keycard. I'll make an excuse, sneak away and get it done."

Ryland wasn't overly worried about palming the room key off Tillman. He'd always been good with his hands and could accomplish the feat in his sleep. His mother had taught him and Addie how to pickpocket from anyone, anywhere, when they were kids. Despite not agreeing with their thieving ways, he'd put the skill to good use a few times before. After finding out their room number, the issue was making up a believable excuse so he could disappear for about fifteen minutes or so, sneak into the room and return to dinner with no one the wiser.

They decided the easiest thing to do was pretend Ryland felt ill from something he'd eaten earlier. He could realistically disappear for up to twenty minutes and then return.

It would work, he decided. No one would question an upset stomach or, God forbid, the dreaded traveler's diarrhea.

******

Later that evening, Ryland sent Jackie a slow, sexy smile full of promise then took a sip of his wine. He was pouring the charm on thick and using every trick in his seductive arsenal to disarm and enchant her. He needed their room number and he and Harper were pouring the sugar on, setting the groundwork for a night of promised sensuality.

The other couple seemed to be taking the bait.

And, although Ryland wanted to dig for information, he knew it was next to impossible considering the scenario. Tillman wasn't sharing his real name and was going by two different aliases. There's no way he'd share anything remotely personal and true about his life in the real world.

So, instead, they laid on the charisma and magnetism and sought the information he needed first and foremost. Thirty minutes later, Ryland grinned broadly when Tillman invited them to his and Jackie's room for a nightcap.

Ryland slid a questioning look in Harper's direction and she nodded. "I think we'd both enjoy that very much," he answered.

"Very much." Harper echoed.

"Wonderful," Jackie said. She'd been eye fucking Ryland all throughout dinner and he tossed her wink. "We're in room 401."

Bull's eye.

Armed with the intel and invitation he needed, Ryland flirted a bit longer, patiently waiting for the right moment. When the time came to make his move, Ryland claimed his stomach was bothering him, excused himself from the table and passed behind Tillman's chair.

"Oh, and sweetheart," Ryland said, stopping…slipping a stealthy hand into the side pocket of Tillman's jacket…smiling at Harper…palming the keycard. "Please, don't let me eat any more pineapple."

Harper giggled and shrugged her shoulders at Tillman and Jackie. "My bad. But it might be worth it later."

"You're always worth it," Ryland said, then walked in the direction of the restroom. Once he was out of their sight, he veered left.

Room 401. Not too far away, but not close either. Ryland picked up his pace, checked his watch and hustled through the lobby, heading for the nearest hallway where the guest rooms started. He jogged forward, determined to make good timing so he could return and save poor Harper from those two sharks. Because they were probably already circling her like chum in the water.

Once he reached 401, he ignored the Do Not Disturb sign and easily opened the door with the stolen keycard. After stepping inside, he quickly closed it and latched the security bar. Tillman and his partner were slobs and he had to step around clothing strewn everywhere, open luggage, scattered shoes, leftover room service and wet towels. The large bed was unmade and they clearly hadn't allowed housekeeping inside.

Scanning over the mess, searching for Tillman's laptop, he spotted it on the side table beside a mug with

218

sludgy, cold coffee still lingering in the bottom. Wrinkling his nose, Ryland sat down on the chair's edge and removed the small external drive from his pocket. After connecting the short USB cord to Tillman's laptop, he initiated the cloning process.

Best case scenario, he could get the job done in ten minutes. Narrowing his eyes as he watched the intel moving over, he realized it would take about seventeen minutes to copy the 100GB hard drive.

"Shit," he mumbled under his breath. It was definitely longer than he wanted, but there was nothing he could do about it.

Ryland just hoped Harper could hang in there and he'd return as soon as possible.

******

With Ryland gone, Harper's level of discomfort skyrocketed. She felt like a gazelle being circled by two hungry lions. Tillman and Jackie made no qualms about letting her know they were ready to play some switch-up games. Harper did her best to act interested and ready to have fun, but inside she wanted to cry. They were creeping her out with their heated looks and she was twisting her napkin in her lap.

Ryland will be back soon, she told herself. *Dig deep and channel Meryl.* Oh, hell, who was she kidding? She needed to channel a porn star.

She just had to hang in there a little longer and then they could get the hell out of there.

******

"Motherfucker!" Ryland hissed. Halfway through copying the hard drive, the computer froze. He didn't have time for this shit. Yanking the cord out, he tried to start the process all over again.

But it wasn't working.

Nostrils flaring, he pulled his phone out of his pocket and called Banshee.

"What's going on, Rip?" Banshee answered.

"It's frozen and I can't get the fucker to re-start."

"Shit. Okay, let me hack into the hotel's Wi-Fi network, try to remote in and see what's going on."

With a frustrated sigh, Ryland ground his teeth together and checked his watch. He'd been gone for almost twenty minutes.

It's okay. Harper can handle it.

At least he hoped so.

******

Tillman and Jackie were growing impatient. They'd finished eating and Harper tried to prolong dinner by suggesting dessert or another glass of wine. But they both declined.

"Freddy should be back soon," Harper said, feigning confidence.

"Maybe, maybe not." Tillman looked at his watch again. "But in the meantime, we could be using our time more wisely. Don't you think?"

Beside him, Jackie nodded. "I'm bored. Maybe we could wait for him in there?" She pointed to a private room where Harper had seen several couples disappear earlier. It was probably one of the resort's infamous sex spots and there was no way she planned on going in there with these two predators ready to devour her.

"I think we should order another round," Harper suggested, trying to act casual. "On me. What do you say?"

"I say we're ready to go to the Playroom and have some fun, Annabelle. Why don't you join us."

Harper hesitated. *No, no, no.* Where the hell was Ryland and why was he taking so long?

"If you're not interested then I'm just going back to the room," Jackie pouted.

"No!" Harper blurted out and they both sent her a funny look. *Relax, Harper. Play it cool. This is all just an act.* "I mean, what exactly is the Playroom? This is my first time visiting here, so sorry if I seem a little nervous."

Her words made them visibly relax and Tillman sent her a wolfish smile.

"It's a room where we can play, sweet girl."

A shiver ran down Harper's spine and she looked down at her lap where she'd shredded her entire napkin into tiny pieces. She didn't want to go in there with them, but if it could buy Ryland some more time then she didn't have a choice.

Looking up, she pasted on a smile and said, "Okay."

"And it's alright to be nervous." Jackie placed a hand over hers. "But don't worry, we'll be gentle since it's your first time."

She and Tillman exchanged a look and smirked.

"Just realize that the Playroom isn't just for watching. You're expected to participate," Tillman added and stood up, beyond ready to go.

Oh, God. Heart thumping madly, Harper slowly stood up. *Ryland, where are you?*

******

"You got it?" Ryland asked.

"Nearly there," Banshee said. "Gimme another few minutes."

222

Raking a hand through his wild, sun-bleached hair, Ryland mentally went through every curse word he could think of. He hoped Harper was charming the hell out of them and not having any trouble stalling their inevitable advances.

Almost done, sweetheart. Hang in there.

He owed her big-time for helping them pull this off and he planned to pay her back with multiple orgasms.

******

Harper didn't know what to expect, but when they stepped into the Playroom, her heart sank. There were several other couples in there and they were definitely, ah, playing. Some were half-clothed, others not so much.

The lighting was dim and there were mattresses up on platforms scattered around the room. Some kind of sex swing hung in a corner, currently occupied by a woman, her legs spread from here to China and a man's head going to town between her thighs.

A fierce blush spread over Harper's cheeks and she was grateful for the low lighting. Good God, what had she stepped into? It was like a scene from some kinky porno flick.

"Why don't we sit down and relax? Let our playroom virgin find her footing, take in the atmosphere," Tillman suggested, leading them to an empty mattress in the corner.

Forcing herself to sit down, Harper breathed a sigh of relief to find the white sheets clean and crisp. At least the place was spotless. Trying to ignore the moans and sounds the other couples were making, Harper pulled in a deep, steadying breath.

Tillman reached over and dragged a good-sized box up onto the mattress, setting it beside him. He flipped the lid and reached inside. Harper swallowed hard when he lifted some type of leather crop out.

"Tell us your fantasies, Harper. BDSM, role playing, girl on girl…What are your hidden yearnings? We'll make them come true."

Jackie removed a large feather and ran it over Harper's thigh. "There's so much we can do. With or without Fred."

"We can start slow. Just take your clothes off and we'll make you feel good."

"Don't be shy," Jackie coaxed. "Let your deepest desires guide you."

Fuck me. Her deepest desires did not involve either of these two, but how far was she willing to take this game? Harper didn't want to break their cover but, at the same time, things were starting to move way too fast.

The situation unfolding was real, not some scene in

acting class meant to test her limits and push her emotions.

Flung so far out of her comfort zone, Harper forced a smile and cast a last, desperate look at the door, praying for Ryland to walk through it and whisk her away.

But it was painfully clear she was on her own.

Across from her Tillman began unbuttoning his shirt and her stomach sank.

Chapter Seventeen

"Done," Banshee finally declared.

The words were barely out of his mouth and Ryland was already yanking the USB cord free and stuffing the drive back into his pocket. He slammed the laptop shut, spun around and raced toward the door.

"Roger that," Ryland said. "I'll be in touch." He hung up, unlatched the security bolt and exited the room.

He'd been gone for almost thirty fucking minutes. *Not good.* Racing down the hallway, he hauled ass through the lobby and then slowed down when he reached the restaurant. The table they'd been sitting at was now empty, the hotel staff resetting it for the next guests.

Fucking hell.

Turning, Ryland's gaze scanned the room. Where had they gone? Maybe down to the bar or to the beach or—

His gaze landed on the Playroom. *No.* She wouldn't have gone in there with them. Would she have?

A niggling sensation in his gut told him to check it out and Ryland skirted around the other diners, determined to look. He knew if he found her in there it wouldn't be for any other reason than to keep up their charade. And the thought of her in what he knew would be an uncomfortable situation heightened his frustration and urged him to move even faster.

Pushing the door open, he squinted against the low lighting, his eyes adjusting, and even though there were other couples—all of them involved in some kind of sex act—his gaze zeroed right in on Harper.

She sat on a mattress facing the half-dressed pair of cougars who were drooling over her. Anger fueled Ryland as he stomped around a fornicating couple, another couple bent into a very weird, pretzel-like pose on a swing, and straight to his woman.

Harper glanced up as he reached the mattress and palpable relief flooded her.

"Ry—" She abruptly stopped herself, his real name on her tongue, and quickly righted herself, patting the place beside her. "Right here, baby."

But Ryland was done playing. He reached down, scooped her into his arms and turned on his heel.

"Hey!" Tillman exclaimed in annoyance. "Where are you going?"

"Find another couple," Ryland growled. "She's mine."

"Oh, thank God," Harper breathed against his neck, her arms wrapped tightly around him, as he stomped out.

Hell, she was hanging on for dear life and Ryland fumed over the fact that he'd left her for so long by herself to fend off the wolves. "I'm so sorry, sweetheart." His hold tightened on her as he stormed straight off the back patio and onto the sand. "We had some technical complications."

"But you got it?"

"We got it," he assured her.

"Oh, good." He felt the anxiety and tension leave her body as she cuddled even closer to him.

Ryland carried her away from the hotel and the havoc it created in his mind. He needed to be alone with her, to make sure she was okay. Once he reached the overhanging branches of a palm tree, he carefully set her down.

"You're okay?" he asked, trying to read her eyes in

the glow of the moonlight.

She nodded. "Yes and you got there just in time."

"Thank Christ," he grunted and pressed a kiss to her forehead. "If he touched you, if he so much as laid one hand on you—"

"He didn't," she assured him before pushing up onto her toes and pressing her lips against his.

His body sagged in relief. They'd gotten what they came for and Harper was safe in his arms. Now, they could celebrate. Finally.

Wrapping his arms around her, Ryland took control of the kiss, forcing her head back, sliding his tongue into her mouth and kissing her passionately. Her coconut-vanilla scent enveloped him, driving him crazy, and he slid his hands under her ass and lifted her up. Harper's legs wrapped around his narrow hips and he pressed her back up against the palm tree, grinding against her, letting her know how much he wanted her.

Being deep inside Harper again was his number one priority and he didn't think he could make it back to the room. He groaned into her mouth when she undulated her hips against his hard, straining dick.

"I need you, sweetheart. So damn badly." Desperation laced his raspy voice and if she kept rubbing against him like that, he was going to burst. He needed to cool off or he was going to embarrass himself.

Turning, Ryland held her tightly to him as he marched down to the water's edge. Without a word, he strode straight into the sea and Harper squealed, wrapping herself tightly around him.

"What're you doing?" she cried and threw her head back with a laugh.

"Putting out some of this fire before it consumes me." The cool ocean did little to ease his desire, though, and he waded deeper. Once the water hit his waist, he slid his hand under her dress and ripped her panties off. Harper gasped, but then his hands were on her and the gasp turned into soft, mewling whimpers as his fingers plunged between her legs and began to tease mercilessly.

"Ryland…" she murmured, fingers digging into his arms.

"Lean back," he ordered and nipped her neck. Harper's aqua gaze, filled with trust, met his and she slowly let herself fall backwards, floating on the waves, legs wrapped around his waist. Exposing herself to him completely.

Ryland's fingers worked her taut, little clit until she was thrusting her hips, rising up and down with each wave, and he sank his finger into her core, followed by another one. She shamelessly rode his hand, her chest heaving with each cry. He could see her pebbled nipples pressing against the sheer fabric of the dress, highlighted by moonlight, and his aching dick lengthened, threatening to tear through his pants.

While he continued to stroke between her legs, his other hand curved over her breast and played with her nipple, lightly pinching it between his fingers.

"Oh, my God, Ryland." She began to twist and writhe, trying to hold back, but it was impossible. He'd taken her right to the edge and now she was slipping over the side, plummeting toward her release. Ecstasy hit her hard, flowing over her face, and her entire body tensed then released. The orgasm left her shaking and he pulled her up, holding her close.

Kissing the side of her face, he tasted the salty wetness and pressed his lips to the curve of her ear. "I'm dying to be inside you," he rasped, "but I don't have anything."

She straightened up in his arms and reached between their bodies, unbuttoning his pants. "I'm protected," she murmured, releasing his aching cock. She lifted herself up, circled her core over his engorged tip, and Ryland groaned long and hard.

Nothing had ever felt so fucking good.

"Are you sure?" he rasped, knees threatening to buckle. If not, he was about to finish himself off right there. He couldn't stand another moment of the pulsing need and the pressure building was too much.

In answer, Harper sank down on his steel length, pulling him deep, and he thrust up hard. There were no words to describe what it felt like. Sinking bare into her hot, wet core and being buried to the hilt as her inner muscles squeezed him. It was heaven.

And if this was what heaven truly felt like, Ryland could die a very happy man.

******

Harper held onto Ryland's shoulders, threw her head back and his name burst from her lips. Maybe she should've been quieter and more discreet, but then she remembered where they were. And, for the first time in her life, she truly let go.

Until Ryland, sex had never been good. It had merely been a humiliating chore that her ex guilt-tripped her into doing then he'd turn around and insult her performance.

But not Ryland. He was pumping into her body like he couldn't get enough of her, hips pistoning, and he wasn't being quiet about it either. His inhibitions and restraint were gone, replaced with a dirty-talking, hot fucking machine.

And she loved it.

"Fuck yeah! You feel that, sweetheart? Feel how

deep I am in you?"

"Yes!" she cried.

"Squeeze me harder. Ohhh, fuuuck. Don't stop."

At that moment, Ryland was as free as she was and their control shattered. Turning, he let the waves hit his back, taking the brunt of their force, and using them to his advantage as he thrust into her.

"Ohmygod," Harper gasped as her body clenched around him, rippling with another orgasm. The way he stretched her body and filled her was like nothing she'd known before. Ryland was hot and thick, expanding her to the point where the pleasure bordered on sweet pain. But he knew how to use his cock, his mouth and his fingers and any discomfort was gone before it began.

"Yeah, just like that. Squeeze that pussy tighter. Milk me hard, Harper. Don't hold back. Fuuuuck," he ground out and buried his face in the curve of her neck and shoulder, shuddering hard.

His hot release filled her and Harper cried out again, her body spasming around him. "Holy shit," she breathed and collapsed against him. She couldn't catch her breath and her heart was beating so damn hard she thought it was in danger of exploding from her chest.

Normally during sex she maintained her composure with relative ease and never lost control. But Ryland yanked that control from her and snapped it in two. It was a bit unnerving but, at the same time, nothing had ever felt so damn good.

Ryland Mills had come into her life and flipped it upside down. Far from just the hot surfer dude she had pegged him as, the former SEAL turned assassin had drawn her into some seriously dangerous shit. But cradled in his arms, sated and breathless after the most incredible sex she'd ever had, she wasn't sure what was more dangerous. The bad men coming after them or the way her heart was opening up to him. The way she wanted, maybe even needed, him on a soul-deep level.

The unnerving part was she was falling so hard, so fast. But how wise was it to get emotionally involved with a man who had deep, endless secrets? A man who had warned her that he wasn't a good person.

At this point, Harper didn't know what was scarier. Falling for Ryland or facing The Agency.

******

They barely made it back to their room after he carried her from the ocean before Ryland had Harper bent over the side of their private jacuzzi, her ass hiked up, as he slammed into her slick body from behind. He was a man possessed and he couldn't get enough of her.

After what happened earlier in the Playroom, he was overcome by the need to mark her. To make her his

234

in every possible way. In every possible position. Tillman had tried to touch her and that unleashed a jealous fury he didn't even know he was capable of feeling.

Harper belonged to him and nobody else.

Tilting her hips just right, he positioned her in front of one of the jets and let the stream of water hit that sweet, little swollen spot he knew would send her over the edge. No doubt about it. She was going to be sore tomorrow and every time she felt a twinge, she'd think of him and how he'd branded her with his cock. And that's exactly what he wanted.

The bubbles broke her and Harper screamed, her body spasming then going limp. The moment after she orgasmed, Ryland came hard enough to bring down the whole damn resort. He roared out his release, collapsing over her, his wet chest pressed to her back.

He buried his face in her soaked hair as small aftershocks left him twitching. Brushing her wet strands of hair aside, he placed a gentle kiss between her shoulder blades and knew one thing for certain: Harper Grant owned him.

And he was not letting her go.

Chapter Eighteen

After spending most of the night fucking each other senseless, Ryland and Harper fell into a deep, satiated sleep. They planned to leave early the next morning, but a call woke them before the alarm did.

With a groan, Ryland reached for his phone and saw Banshee's name flashing on the screen. It was barely seven and he swiped the bar over, grumbling, "This better be important."

"After you sent me the files off Tillman's laptop, I started looking into them. I haven't slept a wink."

"Because you're a robot." Beside him, Harper rolled over with a soft sigh.

"Caffeine, my friend. I live on it."

"You and Bruja."

"So, I found Tillman's calendar and he has a meeting scheduled for today. I've already updated Pharaoh and he wants you to follow Tillman to the meeting place and see if you can sneak onboard and get some intel."

"Onboard?" He rubbed a palm against his eyes.

"It's happening on a yacht just off the coast. In two hours."

"Who's he meeting?"

"Believe it or not, under notes, he wrote T.A. So we figure it's either The Agency or he's scheduled in some tits and ass. Dude has a very limited sense of caution when it comes to his calendar."

"Fuck," Ryland murmured, sitting up. "Send me the details."

"Already on it."

"Thanks, Banshee. I'll report to Pharaoh afterward."

"Roger that."

Ryland disconnected the call, scrubbed a hand over his stubbled jaw and glanced down at Harper who blinked up at him with sleepy eyes.

"What's going on?" she asked.

"Tillman has a meeting on a yacht in two hours with

someone associated with The Agency, and I'm going in to see what I can find out."

Harper popped up, clutching the sheet to her chest. "I'm going with you."

Her voice was firm and Ryland didn't have time to argue with her. Besides, it was just a little bit of recon. Nothing too dangerous. And he'd make sure she stayed far enough away from the yacht to be recognized. It also wouldn't hurt to have an extra set of hands and eyes just in case. "We're going to need a boat. I'm not exactly sure how this is going to go down, but I won't turn down a sexy get-away boat operator."

"You've got it," she assured him.

Damn, she was fearless. Ryland grabbed her face and kissed her hard. "We leave in fifteen minutes."

They got ready quickly and Ryland made sure he had everything he needed in the small waterproof backpack he'd brought along. Since it was still so early and the boat rental places were closed, he and Harper made their way down to the dock where all sorts of water equipment, from small motorboats to wave runners to kayaks, waited for resort guests to use.

Since they couldn't rent, they'd have to borrow.

Slipping around the closed rental shack and ducking out of sight, Ryland pulled his picking tools out of a cargo pants pocket and got to work.

"You're a man of many talents, aren't you?" Harper murmured, blocking him from view and keeping a lookout.

As he worked the lock, he said, "You have no idea, sweetheart."

"They teach you how to pick locks in SEAL training?"

"Nope. That would be courtesy of my mom."

"Your mom?" Harper echoed.

Click. The door opened and Ryland motioned for her to follow him inside. "Long story better saved for later." He had no idea what possessed him to spill that little tidbit, but he was glad he did. Maybe confiding in her about Addie and his mom would help because keeping it all bottled up wasn't doing him any good.

Ryland walked straight over to a pegboard covered in hanging keys and plucked one off that belonged to a motorboat. Key in hand, they left the rental shack and walked down to the boats bobbing up and down in the waves. Acting as if they belonged there. Confidence was key and, lucky for Ryland, he had a lot of it.

"That one," he said and pointed to a boat that matched the number on the key. After helping Harper step inside, he jumped aboard, untied the ropes that secured it to the dock and started the motor. Then he consulted the GPS on his large watch, turned them in the right direction and hit the throttle.

Since it was still early, there wasn't a ton of traffic on the water. Bouncing over the waves, Ryland snuck a glance at Harper as he gave her a quick rundown on how the boat operated, and his heart skipped a beat. The angle of the sun highlighted her perfectly, creating an ethereal halo effect around her beautiful face. His gaze dropped to briefly admire the rest of her, and he thought she looked like some kind of enchanting sea temptress. A siren or mermaid maybe. Damn, those short shorts of hers would be his undoing.

Dragging his attention back to the GPS, he followed it until a yacht came into view.

"There it is!" Harper pointed to the multi-million-dollar behemoth anchored in the distance. "Wow."

Yeah, wow was an understatement. The Sea Nymph was an incredible water toy and boasted an opulence and luxury only achievable by superyachts. From the intel Banshee sent, Ryland knew no expense was spared when the ship was built. It boasted a glass-bottomed swimming pool on the main deck which illuminated the clubroom below, a stunning, specially-designed Swarovski crystal masterpiece that hung in the main salon for diners to admire as it caught sunlight, and a high level of privacy and security, including a drone defense system.

But Ryland wasn't worried in the least because he had one very important thing the Sea Nymph and its crew didn't.

He had Banshee.

Tapping the tiny comms in his ear, he said, "Eyes on the target."

"Roger that, Rip." Pharaoh's voice came through loud and clear as though his team leader were standing right beside him and not actually thousands of miles away. "Proceed to the port side. Banshee hacked into their system and has eyes on everything. Proceed to the southern corridor and the meeting is happening in the third room on the left, facing the ocean, so watch your six and stay below eye level."

"Roger," Ryland said and dropped anchor. Then he reached back, pulled his shirt off and slipped the backpack over his shoulders. He swapped his deck shoes for flippers and decided to swim over in his shorts rather than wear that hideous speedo again.

Harper watched him closely, worrying her lower lip.

"Everything will be fine," he assured her. Then he pressed a hard, fast kiss to her lips, laying a hand over hers where she clutched a two-way radio tightly. If she saw anything alarming or suspicious, she would call and warn him.

241

"Be careful," she whispered fiercely.

"This is child's play." When she lifted a concerned brow, he sent her a cocky smirk. "It's me in the ocean. What could possibly go wrong?"

"Please, don't tempt fate."

"I got this." After another quick kiss, he threw one long leg over the side, followed by the other, and dropped into the ocean.

With strong, smooth strokes, Ryland swam toward the yacht. He would've loved to have some scuba gear, but they hadn't had time to steal that, too. Fortunately, he could hold his breath for a long time, so once he was within range of the stern, he pulled in a deep lungful of air and dove beneath a wave.

Approaching underwater kept him out of sight and he slowly broke the surface exactly three minutes later right next to the boat. Treading water, Ryland tapped his comms and reported in. "I'm alongside the yacht. Banshee, do you see anyone near the swim platform?"

"Negative. And cameras in the south corridor are looping. You're clear, Rip."

"Roger." Ryland pulled himself onto the platform, removed the flippers and stashed them beneath a bench. After giving his head a shake, he grabbed a towel from the shelf and quickly wiped his body down. The last thing he wanted to do was leave a watery trail in his wake.

Tossing the towel into a bin, he stalked forward, not bothering to pull out his Glock. He needed his hands free and didn't anticipate any problems. At the same time, he wasn't arrogant enough to not have a backup plan.

Backup plans had saved his life on more than one occasion.

Sticking close to the wall, he moved forward on silent, bare feet, counting doors until he spotted the maintenance closet and ducked inside. Dropping into a squat, he slid the backpack off his shoulders, unzipped it and pulled out a minuscule fiber optic camera.

God, he loved the toys he was able to play with.

Banshee's voice crackled in his ear. "I've got eyes on Tillman. He just arrived and is boarding now. The south corridor is clear and you're good to go."

"Roger that," Ryland responded in a low voice, replacing the backpack on his shoulders and standing back up. Opening the closet door, he slipped out and made his way up the hallway, ignoring the cameras above him that Banshee had put on a loop.

When he reached the room next door to where the meeting would be taking place, he slipped inside and got to work. Dropping down on his belly in front of the vent, Ryland extended the small, steel pole and slid the camera through the slats.

If everything went according to plan, Ryland would get the entire meeting recorded with sound. "Fiber optic cam is hot," he murmured.

"Okay, we're live," Banshee reported.

"Going for audio."

"Audio confirmed. Tillman is approaching the room, but I don't see our mystery guest yet."

"He's coming," Ryland said calmly. The contact from The Agency had to be there to meet Tillman or what would be the point of this? They weren't even sure who owned the superyacht because it was listed under an umbrella corporation with multiple subsidiaries, and Banshee was still digging for that tidbit.

But Ryland had a feeling they were about to find out.

A moment later, the door opened, and Ryland watched as a bulky man, clearly armed, escorted Tillman inside and motioned for him to sit down at the large conference room table. Once Tillman was seated, the other man immediately exited, closing the door behind him.

After the security guard left, Ryland waited patiently as Tillman set his briefcase on the table, unlatched it and removed a laptop. Then he began typing.

244

Since Tillman sat at an angle, Ryland couldn't get the laptop's screen on camera. But he could pick up sound and when a man greeted Tillman, Ryland leaned forward, listening closely to their exchange.

"When will you be back in the country?" the mysterious man asked, voice sounding displeased. "We have five loose ends to eliminate and you're flitting around in the Caribbean."

"I understand that, Mr. Smith, and I assure you we're working on it. We didn't expect them to escape Abu Dhabi or the mercs sent to take them out."

"Clearly, you're underestimating them and that makes you a fool. This team is the best of the best. Have you forgotten that?"

Tillman hung his head like a scolded dog. "No, sir. We also sent the best of the best to handle the situation."

"Really? Because only one of Ex Nihilo is down. What the fuck are you waiting for?" he growled.

"Cipher assured us—"

"Don't blame anyone else for your error in judgment or incompetence," Mr. Smith snapped. "I don't like when people fail me and I will only tolerate it for so long. Do I make myself clear?"

"Yes," Tillman practically whined. Then he perked up. "Maybe we alter the plan—send in the Cardinal now?"

For a moment, the other man didn't respond. "No," he finally said. "The Cardinal is a last resort."

"Fine," Tillman ground out, clearly unhappy. "The call's been put in to the Merciers and we're waiting for their response."

"I suggest you figure it out fast because if you don't get the situation resolved soon, don't be surprised to find your name added to our list."

"Understood. I won't let you down."

Cipher, the Cardinal, the Merciers…

Who the hell are all these people? Ryland wondered as they finished their virtual meeting. And was Lester Tillman really a member of The Agency? Because Mr. Smith seemed to be the one in charge while Tillman seemed more like an underling. Could Banshee's list of names be wrong? Was there more to it than what he'd uncovered so far?

After once again ensuring Mr. Smith that he would take care of everything, Tillman politely said goodbye. Once Smith disconnected the call, Tillman slammed the laptop closed and cursed loudly.

Ryland carefully retracted the small pole and detached the camera. He folded it up and stashed everything back in his pack. Time to get the hell out of

246

there. But first, he had to wait for security to escort Tillman off the ship. Then he'd make a break for it and return to Harper.

"Rip!" Banshee's voice vibrated through his comms loudly. "They discovered the looping footage and cams are back up! You need to get out of there now!"

Funny how things never went as planned.

Chapter Nineteen

Shit. Ryland hadn't been compromised yet, but the second he stepped into the hallway, he knew they'd see him on the CCTV footage. Spinning around, he jogged over to check out the window situation. Maybe he could jump out and swim back.

A quick scan told him they were sealed shut. For decoration and light only. *No way out there.* Ryland moved back over to the door, pulled it open a crack and looked out. A security team of five was heading up the south corridor, opening doors and checking rooms as they made their way forward.

"Sonofabitch." Ryland reached for his two-way radio and did the only thing he could do. He called Harper, his Plan B. Keeping the volume and his voice low, he hissed, "Harper? Do you copy?"

There was a slight crackle and she immediately responded. "I copy. What's happening?"

"I need a distraction, sweetheart. Can you drive that boat over here and cause a really fucking big one? Because cams are up and I need to jump onto that boat with you."

A brief, silent pause met his ears. Then, "Yes. Hang on, Ryland, I'm coming."

******

"Shit! Shit! Shit!"

Harper turned the key in the boat's ignition and crossed her fingers. She'd never driven a boat before in her life and she tried to calm her mind as she recalled what Ryland had shown her on their way out. She also kept picturing that scene from *Weekend at Bernie's* when the characters couldn't get the boat out of the harbor and realized only too late that boats don't have brakes.

But they definitely had a throttle and Harper hit it hard. Ryland needed her and she wasn't going to let him down. As she plowed over the waves, heading straight for the superyacht as fast as she could, she tried not to think too hard about how she planned on stopping the motorboat.

******

Everything seemed to happen at once.

A security guard opened the door where Ryland was waiting and, using the element of surprise, he grabbed the guard, overpowering him, and dragged him down to the floor in a chokehold. The second the man passed out, Ryland jumped up and moved into the doorway.

Glock in hand, he peered out and came face to face with fucking Tillman. *Goddammit.*

"Fred?" Tillman's eyes widened and he looked past Ryland, most likely searching for Harper, aka Annabelle Rogers. "What're you doing here?"

He looked so utterly baffled that Ryland could only roll his eyes. Not wasting time on Tillman, Ryland focused on the four guards who just spotted him. "No time to chat, John. See you and Jackie back at the resort!"

"Drinks later?" Tillman called out, voice hopeful.

Christ. What a creep. Ryland ran down the corridor, turning the corner and skidding outside just in time to see the motorboat plow into the yacht's rear swim platform.

There she was, right on time. His woman had come crashing in to rescue him.

Ryland quickly retrieved his flippers and took a running leap off the end of the yacht. He sailed through the air, landing in a crouch on the motorboat.

"I didn't know how to stop it!" Harper yelled, throwing her arms up.

"You did good!" he assured her, wrapping an arm around her waist and planting a quick kiss on her lips. "Brilliant distraction, sweetheart."

"I didn't even get to my actual distraction."

"Oh?" Luckily, there wasn't any significant damage to either boat and Ryland jumped into the captain's seat and spun the wheel. "And what was that?"

Shoving the throttle forward, he guided them away from the yacht, heading toward a cluster of cliffs.

"I was going to flash them," she announced cheekily.

"Oh, hell." That definitely would've worked and he was glad he'd made it out fast enough, so she hadn't needed to do it. Right now, they needed to ditch the boat and—

"Ryland! They're coming after us!"

Ryland glanced over his shoulder and saw two speed boats being lowered into the water. There's no way they could outrun those things. At this point, their best hope would be to reach the cliffs ahead where they could ditch the boat and hide. Lucky for them, Jamaica's landscape stemmed from its volcanic nature and a large limestone plateau covered most of the island. This meant there were hundreds of caves and caverns scattered all over the place which pirates had taken advantage of back

251

in the day to hide their loot.

And now Ryland and Harper could hide themselves.

The steep rock face with endless crags loomed closer and closer. There were infinite crevices and coves where they could slip into and easily lose the thugs tailing them. However, they'd be dangerous, too, and they'd have to be careful. It would suck to outrun the men chasing them only to impale their small vessel on a sunken ship's mast. Or get lost or injured in the labyrinth of tunnels dotting the area.

It didn't take long to reach one of the sheltered coves and Ryland let the boat glide right up against the rocks. "C'mon. Let's lose these assholes."

He reached for Harper's hand and helped her over the side and onto a large rock. After he hopped out, he looked back to see their pursuers were gaining ground fast. Far too fast for comfort, and he tugged Harper with him.

"Careful not to slip," he said, hurrying forward, gaze searching for the perfect place to hide. They moved quickly, skirting along huge boulders and sharp rock walls until he finally found a cave that looked promising.

Leaving the bright sunshine behind, they moved into the dank cavern, winding along a narrow ledge and heading into the gloom beyond. The water was high, lapping over the edge, and their feet were getting wet.

Harper's fingers tightened around Ryland's hand and she hesitated.

"Just a little further," Ryland coaxed. "They won't come back here. It's too dangerous with the tide coming in."

At least, that's what he was betting on.

******

The tide was rising extremely fast, and no one in their right mind would go this deep into the dark cave. It was far too treacherous and getting harder to navigate. Harper's foot slipped and she gasped, quickly covering her mouth to stifle the sound.

"You're okay," Ryland said, gripping onto her more tightly.

They'd reached the back of the cavern just as a large wave came rolling through and washed up onto their ledge, soaking the bottom half of their legs. Harper felt a surge of panic, watching as the water rose faster than she imagined possible. She'd never been a strong swimmer and rarely ventured any deeper than her waist in a large body of water.

Drowning was not on her to-do list today. She reminded herself she was with a Navy SEAL and he was a strong swimmer. He was also smart, intuitive and capable. She knew she could trust him to keep her safe.

However, she didn't trust the tide that seemed to be getting dangerously stronger and more threatening.

The sounds of men talking echoed through the air and Ryland pulled Harper deeper into the corner. Too scared to move, much less breathe, she froze and listened. It was impossible to tell where their pursuers actually were in the cave system because of the crazy acoustics and constant roar of the waves. So their only choice was to wait it out and hope the bad guys either left or chose to explore a different cavern.

The sea water kept creeping higher and higher, and the moment it hit her knees, Harper's fight or flight mode kicked in hard. She wanted to get the hell out of there. Once high tide hit, they had no idea if the whole cave would be submerged.

But if they attempted to leave now, they would most likely run into the guys from the yacht who were all sporting some awfully big guns.

Forcing herself to breathe, Harper clutched onto Ryland's arm, trying to control the panic rising hard and fast.

He laid his hand over hers, straining to hear. A large wave crashed through the cave, hitting the back wall, soaking them, and Ryland cursed. Harper was a beat away from a panic attack and dug deep, biting her lip hard and blinking away the salty water dripping from her eyelashes.

"Hold onto me," he ordered her in a low voice. "And don't let go."

"Ryland—" Another wave slammed into them and Ryland turned, taking the brunt of the impact with the side of his body. His long fingers were wedged into a rocky crevice and that was the only thing anchoring them from being pummeled around the chamber.

Harper did not want to fall off the ledge and she prayed Ryland had a good grip. If the waves knocked them off, they'd get battered fiercely then probably swept out to sea. Or worse. She knew the undertow would be dangerous and if it held them underwater or if they got caught on the bottom…

Her heart stuttered. The water was up to her waist now and she could hear another big wave roaring toward them. Turning her face against Ryland's chest, her arms snaked around his narrow waist, and she sucked in a deep breath, preparing herself for the inevitable battering.

But nothing could ready her for the vicious power that hit them. Despite holding on as hard as she could, Harper's grip broke loose and she was swept away from Ryland, caught in a spinning, watery vortex.

******

The moment he felt Harper slip away, Ryland let go of the rocks with one hand and made a mad grab to catch her. Their fingers brushed, missed, and he watched in horror as she was carried away from him. Her blonde head went underwater and the powerful current sucked her backwards.

And she hadn't cried out or screamed, refusing to alert the men hunting them down.

He had to save her. Yet, he knew the power of the ocean better than anyone and jumping into that maelstrom could be suicide. The heavy weight of the water, holding you down, refusing to let go. The first taste of the sea as it washed down the back of your throat. Those were unforgettable horrors.

During his ten years as a frogman, Ryland had almost drowned once. His team had been battling rough waters and their zodiac hit a wave hard enough to toss him over the side. The enormous waves had been brutal and punishing, thrashing him around like a kernel in a popcorn machine. It wasn't easy for his brothers to reach him because the water had been so rough, but one of his teammates had wrapped a rope around himself, battled the ocean's fury, and dragged Ryland back onto the boat. He must've coughed up a bucket of water.

Right now, there was no zodiac to climb back onboard and no rope to secure him. It was just him against the pounding surf, which was way too high to be comfortable.

Avoiding the men hunting them down had been his top priority, but now it was saving Harper.

Ryland let go of the rock, pushed himself off the cavern wall and let the dangerous, swirling water suck him away. *Fuck.* The current was even worse than he originally thought. After inhaling a deep breath, he let it drag him straight down to the bottom. Staying below the pounding surf would be better than trying to stay afloat and fighting it.

His hip slammed against the surprisingly smooth but slippery rock on the cavern floor. The fact that nothing grew on the seabed was a testament to the power of the surf in the caves. And a reminder of exactly what level of force Ryland and Harper were now facing.

Turning around, Ryland conserved his strength and energy by allowing the current to pull him forward. He scanned from right to left, searching for Harper, but the water was so dark he couldn't see a damn thing.

There was the possibility she'd already been spit out of the cave and he began to kick, trying to move faster. Already, it felt like he was stuck in wild rapids, and he spiraled several times, completely out of control.

Ryland managed to grab a small, rocky handhold, and stopped his crazy spin. His lungs were beginning to burn and he clawed his way to the surface. His head broke through and he looked around, but no sign of Harper.

No, no, no. His gut churned and he swiped his wet hair back. Where the hell was she? Harper had come running to his rescue without a second thought for her safety and now it was his turn to rescue her.

And he was failing miserably.

******

Harper felt like she was tumbling around in a washing machine. Every time she managed to right herself, another wave tore through the narrow cavern's tunnel and she got sucked under and began to somersault, head over heels.

Ironic because that's exactly how she felt about Ryland. He'd swept into her world and flipped it completely upside down. But she wouldn't have changed a damn thing.

Even if that meant she was going to die right now.

Because spending the past week with Ryland had been the highlight of her life. He showed her how she deserved to be treated and he worshipped her like no one ever had before. The kindness, playfulness and fierce protection he'd shown her meant so very much.

Harper had been hurt badly by her ex and Ryland was like some magic eraser who came in and wiped all the hurt, anger and bitterness away. She was so incredibly grateful to him and, more than anything, she wanted to tell him what he meant to her.

But fear had held her back and now regret poured

through her.

Harper hadn't planned on drowning today, but sometimes fate had other things in store.

Lungs screaming, body bruised and fingers cut from trying to hold onto the sharp rocks, Harper had two options: give up or fight like hell.

And she decided to fight.

Lungs burning from the lack of oxygen, she kicked hard, using the last of her strength, and attempted to swim to the surface. Right before her head broke through, another massive wave plowed through the cavern and she went tumbling backwards, out of control and out of breath.

Before she could right herself, Harper's head slammed against a rock jutting up from the floor. And everything went black.

******

Ryland prided himself on his ability to control his emotions, especially while on a mission. But now, a sick panic began coursing through his veins. He still didn't see Harper anywhere. He also didn't see their pursuers, and he wasn't sure if that was a good thing or a bad thing.

The worst of the high tide was over and the sea level was beginning to drop again. Ryland swam forward, kicking hard and using powerful strokes to cut through the water. He wanted to yell for Harper, but he didn't want to draw unwanted attention and guns. Because right now they were like two flopping fish in a barrel. Vulnerable and easy to take out.

He was nearing the mouth of the cavern when he saw her floating face down on the surface, blonde hair spread out around her.

Ryland's heart crashed against his chest and he swam harder and faster than he ever had in his life. *Harper!* his mind screamed. This couldn't be happening. She wasn't moving, just rising and falling with the surf.

Please, no. Don't take her from me.

They hadn't had enough time together. There was so much he wanted to do with her. Things he wanted to tell her. Like how he knew from the first moment he laid eyes on her that she was different from every other woman who had ever crossed his path.

He'd seen a future with her flash before his eyes. And that had scared the shit out of him. It was the reason it had been so hard for him to ask her out. He was scared to fuck it up. And now he'd done more than just fuck it up.

He'd failed her.

Finally reaching her, Ryland grabbed Harper in a rescue hold and swam over to the rocks. He seized hold of an outcropping and hauled himself and her out of the suddenly calmer waters. Laying Harper down on her back, his old training surfaced, and he automatically started going through the steps he'd learned in the Navy.

Check for breath. Her chest wasn't moving which meant she wasn't breathing. Slapping two fingers on her neck, he found a weak pulse. He didn't know exactly how long she'd been underwater, but the whole episode had been less than five minutes, and he needed to get her breathing again. That was most important. And that meant performing CPR with rescue breaths.

Dropping down, Ryland carefully tilted her head back and gave five initial rescue breaths before starting the cycle of chest compressions which would hopefully clear her airways and expel any water. After performing thirty compressions, he checked to see if she was breathing.

Nothing.

Godfuckingdammit. She was so cold and her normally flushed face was blue. His heart clenched and cold fear trickled through him.

First his father. Then his mother. Then Tanner. Now Harper. It was like an endless nightmare on repeat. The people he cared about the most dying, leaving him alone.

Ryland grit his teeth, determined to bring her back, and performed two more rescue breaths.

"C'mon, sweetheart. Don't do this to me. *Please*," he begged and started more compressions. The dark part of himself laughed and scoffed, telling him this was exactly what he deserved. After all the people he killed, it was karma that those he loved should be taken away. It didn't matter that he'd been following orders or at one point even had noble intentions about saving the world from bad guys.

It all boiled down to one thing—Ryland was an assassin. He had been in one way or another since he'd been eighteen, enlisted and been trained to kill.

The woman he'd fallen in love with was gone. And it was all his fault. He never should've approached her, much less caught her up in his chaotic world. He'd never forgive himself.

With an agonized roar, Ryland fisted his hand, ready to pound it against her chest, when she suddenly coughed up a mouthful of water.

Relief like he'd never known before flooded through him and he rolled her onto her side, keeping her airway open, letting the water spill out.

"Jesus Christ," he rasped, dropping his head, unable to believe how close he'd been to losing her.

Gathering her in his arms, needing to feel her breathing, Ryland pulled her onto his lap and wrapped his arms around her shivering body.

"You're okay. I've got you." He stroked a hand over her wet hair and pressed his forehead against hers, whispering, "I'm so sorry."

Harper pulled back, her aqua eyes looking up at him through water-spiked lashes. "Sorry for saving me?" The strain on her vocal cords caused her to cough again.

Ryland merely shook his head, at a loss. "You're so damn brave." He cupped her face and stared at her in relieved amazement. She was safe, she was breathing, she was alive.

Thank Christ.

"Baby..." he breathed, unable to stop touching her. Needing to reassure himself that she was there in his arms and he wasn't merely dreaming. He almost lost her, and there would've been no coming back from that kind of devastation.

She's okay, he kept repeating in his head.

"I am never letting you go," he rasped. "You're mine and I'm yours. I fucking love you, Harper. So damn much. Don't you ever drown on me again."

A half laugh, half sob escaped Harper's throat as she wound her arms around his neck. "I won't. And I fucking love you right back. So very much."

Chapter Twenty

Harper was safe, her arms wrapped around Ryland, and she breathed in his clean scent. He helped her up, guided her away from the caves and they spotted the rental boat banging up against a cluster of rocks near the shoreline. After making sure the coast was clear, Ryland climbed over the boulders and hopped into the boat. He maneuvered it over and pulled Harper up inside.

They determined the bad guys had left or were continuing their search elsewhere. And thank God for that because Harper was done. It had been enough excitement for one morning.

On the way back to the hotel, Ryland kept Harper tucked close on his lap, his warm embrace blocking the wind. Still, she shivered. Probably more so from her near-death experience rather than their wet clothes.

It was a relief when they finally reached the resort. Once they were back in the suite, Ryland called Pharaoh and brought him up to date on everything that had happened. Harper shivered when he got to the part about her being swept away and drowning.

Because she hadn't nearly drowned. Harper had actually breathed water into her lungs and stopped breathing. Although she didn't remember what happened after she blacked out, the moments right before it had been terrifying. Especially when she thought she'd never be in Ryland's arms again. Never run her fingers through his hair, look into his striking eyes, feel his lips on hers.

After changing into dry clothes and quickly packing up, they hightailed it over to the private jet. Ryland fawned over her the entire flight back to Mexico, making sure she had whatever she needed. But mostly, she just needed to be near him and to feel his warmth.

After landing in Rosarito, they climbed back into the SUV and Ryland drove them back to their little row of bungalows on the beach. The team had a lot to discuss and Harper was tired, exhausted actually, even after dozing on the flight home. But it was still early evening, and she didn't want to leave Ryland's side. Even though he encouraged her to go to bed and get some rest, she said she'd rather go with him to his team's meeting. If that was okay.

"Of course, it's okay, sweetheart," he murmured

265

and kissed her. "Wherever I go, you're always invited. I want you by my side."

Hand-in-hand, they walked over to Banshee and Bruja's place, entering to a round of enthusiastic and relieved greetings. The team hugged Harper—she was pretty sure she heard a very Ryland-sounding growl when Saint casually wrapped his arms around her—and fist-bumped Ryland. She didn't see Cross anywhere and somehow wasn't surprised. After the warm welcome, everyone gathered around the coffee table in the small living room that overlooked the ocean and got down to business.

"Welcome back," Pharaoh said, his tone deep and commanding like always, reminding her they were back to business. "First things first. Mayhem's funeral is in two days in San Diego, so we'll be driving back tonight." He glanced down at his watch. "As soon as this meeting is over."

Harper squeezed Ryland's hand, knowing the next couple of days were going to be difficult for him, but she'd be by his side every step of the way.

"Next order of business is admitting we're up against a serious enemy. Tillman's meeting with Mr. Smith provided clear confirmation that their main objective is to hunt us down, one by one, until we're eliminated."

"Tillman is a fool," Ryland said, and Harper

nodded. "But he must have a purpose or they wouldn't keep him around."

Harper looked around the room, from one member of Ryland's team to another, and Selma Santiago's warning about one of them being a traitor echoed through her head. Her gut was saying Santiago was a liar, but the possibility couldn't be ruled out yet.

"I still don't understand why." Bruja played with her nunchucks, swinging them around with lethal skill. "What did we do to wind up on their kill list? Because I have to say, I didn't believe a word out of Santiago's mouth."

No one had an answer and Pharaoh shrugged a wide shoulder.

"All I know is we need more help. Someone trustworthy to take Mayhem's spot on the team."

Ryland tensed beside Harper. "Tanner. His name was Tanner."

"It's nothing personal, Rip. Mayhem—Tanner— was an essential part of the team. He will be missed and mourned. But we're down one member, and we can't afford to be. We don't want The Agency to think they're winning. The truth is, we need manpower. Defeating them is going to be really fucking hard. Any ideas on who we can recruit?"

Saint scoffed. "Right. Please, come join my team. Glamorous locations. Beautiful women. Tropical fruit by the bucketload. And, by the way, some powerful group is picking us off and you're likely to be shot dead by next week."

"No one in their right mind is going to join us," Ryland stated, his thumb gently circling the back of Harper's hand.

For a long moment, no one said anything. Then Banshee adjusted his dark-rimmed glasses and leaned forward, clasping his hands between his legs. "What if he's not in his right mind?"

"What're you talking about?" Saint asked.

Pharaoh crossed his muscular forearms and arched a brow. "Who?"

"I may know just the guy. But he comes with baggage."

"Don't we all?" Ryland asked.

Banshee pulled in a breath. "His name's Gray and he used to be on my SEAL team. Demon and I were on Gold Squadron together for a year and got pretty close."

Ryland sat up straighter. "I knew some Knights. Good guys."

Banshee nodded. "Once the Navy found out where

my true talents lie, they exchanged my flippers for computers. I got moved and Demon started working with another team, doing really tough missions. The ones no one else wanted. The 'we don't know you and no one is coming to your rescue if you fail' type."

"Ghost ops?" Pharaoh asked and Banshee nodded.

A shiver ran through Harper. Who would want a job where your own country would forsake you? And what kind of person would be nicknamed Demon?

"He can be a little moody sometimes. Kinda like you, Saint," Banshee said, and Saint flipped him off. "But, overall, a strong ally and powerful warrior. He's loyal, too."

"So what's his baggage?" Pharaoh asked, cutting straight to the chase.

"PTSD and depression mostly. But the main thing is he lost his entire team when a mission went sideways. He was the lone survivor and he's had a rough time re-adjusting to civilian life."

"Fuck," Ryland grumbled sympathetically.

"Is he capable of handling this?" Pharaoh asked.

"I think he'd jump at the chance. Last I heard from a buddy, Demon was rotting away in some trailer up near L.A., wishing he were dead."

"Sounds like a loose cannon to me," Saint commented.

"He's the best of the best," Banshee insisted. "And that's what we need."

When no one said anything, Bruja finally spoke up. "It can't hurt to check him out, right? He might not even be interested, but…it guts me when a warrior gives up. Maybe we can help him find his purpose again."

They all nodded.

"Let's put it to a vote," Pharaoh said diplomatically. "All in favor of checking out Gray?"

"Hooyah," Ryland immediately said.

"Hooyah," Banshee echoed, and Harper smiled as the two men slapped hands over her head.

"Hooah!" Bruja called out enthusiastically.

"Hooah," Pharaoh said in agreement. His lack of enthusiasm made them all snort with laughter.

Bruja punched his arm. "Loosen up a little. I swear, Pharaoh, other than keeping us all alive, you are making it my mission to get your ass laid."

"Leave my ass out if it, please," Pharaoh said in a stilted voice.

"But it's such a fine ass," Bruja teased and they all

snickered.

He huffed out a breath. "What the hell, Bruja? For all you know, I have a wife at home."

The rest of the team exchanged looks and they all said a resounding "no" at the same time then laughed again.

Everyone turned in Saint's direction, waiting for his response. He shrugged a shoulder. "Why the fuck not? Just may want to let the sorry bastard know it could be a suicide mission."

The broody man's words didn't give Harper any comfort and she hoped he was wrong.

Banshee nodded. "Since we'll be back in Cali, we may as well go up to L.A. and drop in on him. You guys might change your mind. Hell, I may, too. We haven't spoken in maybe eight months, and I have no idea what condition he's in."

"We'll find him, evaluate the situation and make our final decision," Pharaoh said, and everyone nodded their agreement.

Ryland sat forward in his seat, like he was about to stand, then surveyed the room and asked, "Where's my dad?"

******

The drive back to San Diego was uneventful and the closer they got, the heavier Ryland's chest grew. Almost to the point where it felt like someone was standing on it. Before leaving, the team had returned to Cross's bungalow and he'd said goodbye to his father in private. But something was nagging at him about their final conversation.

Ever since finding out his dad was still alive, Ryland had experienced mixed emotions. From shock and disbelief to hurt and anger to betrayal and finally acceptance. Currently, he still had no idea where they stood or if it was possible to rebuild their relationship. It felt like they were straddling a fault line and the tectonics were steady for the moment. But if the Big One hit, their tentative foundation would crumble.

As the Suburban cruised up the 405N, Ryland thought back over their parting words.

"You can't go back. That's suicide."

"I have to go to my best friend's funeral," Ryland said between gritted teeth. Something that should've needed zero explanation.

"That'll be the first place they'll look. Don't be stupid, Ryland."

"Have you forgotten what it feels like to lose a brother?"

"He wasn't your brother."

"What?"

"I mean, not technically. He wasn't on your SEAL team."

"Semantics," Ryland snapped. "We were teammates, he was my brother and I'll be there to punch his coffin with my Trident."

"How well do you know your team, Ryland?"

"What?" He didn't like that question for a number of reasons. His dad damn well knew The Agency didn't want them exchanging personal information or getting too friendly with each other. It was part of the contract they all signed, including, he assumed, their handler.

"Think about it. Other than Tanner, who is everyone else? What are their real names? Where do they live?" When Ryland didn't respond, his dad arched a dark brow. "Think about it hard. I know you were told to trust each other and work as a team, but who gave you that directive?"

The Agency. The Agency fucking gave them that directive.

"Trusting your team is comparable to trusting The Agency."

"Bullshit," Ryland growled.

273

"Is it? Or is it an ingenious way to plant a mole?"
He shrugged. "Food for thought."

And since they'd left Mexico, it had been all Ryland could think about. Was his dad right? Aware of something that Ryland wasn't? If that were true, why be so mysterious about it? Why not just be straight and come right out and say who the mole was?

If there even was one.

Unless he didn't know.

Could one of his own team be up to something and on the verge of bringing the rest of them down with a betrayal?

Harper was tucked under his arm, sleeping, and after placing a light kiss against her temple, he looked around the SUV, surreptitiously studying the others. Banshee drove and Bruja sat in the passenger seat beside him. They'd been arguing over the music and flipping back and forth between stations for over an hour. Finally, they'd stumbled upon a song they both approved of and now were currently singing an off-key duet.

To his right, Pharaoh had his large arms crossed and looked deep in thought, most likely prepping for their encounter with Gray. Sometimes, Ryland wondered if the man ever "turned off." His intense nature could be a bit much, but that's also what made him such a good leader. If he hadn't been spec ops of some kind, Ryland would be shocked.

Behind them, Saint lay stretched out on the rear seat. He had ear buds in and was probably listening to one of his podcasts. The man was obsessed with them. Though he hid it well, Saint's slight accent made Ryland think over the sketchy history he'd shared earlier. The FSS? *Fuck.* Russian Intelligence was no joke.

Selma Santiago's final words filled his head and goosebumps broke out over his skin.

"It was determined your team can't be trusted."

"Why not?"

"Because one or more of you is a traitor. Tell me, how well do you know the people you work with?"

Two people had warned him against one of his own teammates. And he didn't fucking like it or want to believe it. But truthfully, the only person he fully trusted with his life right now was Harper.

Squeezing her closer, he pressed a soft kiss to her head and thanked his lucky stars she'd stomped over to his place, demanding answers, after he'd stood her up.

Love you, sweetheart.

Chapter Twenty-One

Grayson "Demon" Ellis

It never rained in Los Angeles in June.

Gray slouched down in the busted-up lawn chair under the torn cloth awning of his trailer. It flapped in the wind above him, and rain like he hadn't seen in ages pounded down from the heavens, soaking the gravel. If it didn't let up soon, the flooding and mudslides would inevitably start. The city couldn't handle massive amounts of rain that fell too fast.

The rainfall made his scar itch and he absently rubbed at the five-inch-long white slash that stretched down his inner forearm. Memories he'd been fighting back all day began to assault him and the only way he knew how to cope was to make himself numb.

Every time it rained like this, he did the only thing he could. He got stinking drunk.

Finishing off his fifth beer, Gray waited for the buzz of indifference to kick in, but it didn't come. Granted, it usually took quite a few beers because he was a big guy. Far from a lightweight at six foot four and nearly two-hundred and twenty pounds of solid muscle, he sometimes was tempted to drown his pain in something stronger like other guys he'd known.

Just crush and snort some hydrocodone and oxycodone. He had a bottle of fentanyl in his cabinet, legally prescribed, but every time he shook out a handful of pills, he ended up putting them back. His buddy died of a fentanyl overdose and Gray didn't want to go out that way.

If he decided to take his life, he'd do it in a blaze of glory, not convulsing on the floor in a pile of his own vomit and piss.

As a former Navy SEAL, he still had standards to maintain. *Yeah, right.* He laughed and it sounded rusty, unused. He couldn't remember the last time he'd been genuinely happy. No, wait, that wasn't true.

It was the day he received his Trident pin.

What a joke. Irony at its best.

If only he knew then what he knew now. How his

career choice would give him the highest and lowest points of his life.

There was no denying he was made to be a SEAL. Despite his size, he was fast and nimble. He worked well under pressure and didn't hesitate to pull the trigger. And, most importantly, he was a team player and always had his buddies' backs.

Until he didn't.

Gray sighed, doing his best to fight the horrific memories he tried so damn hard to keep locked up. But tonight they were leaking out, soaking his brain in their toxicity, dragging him down to drown in the pain.

Dropping his empty bottle, he threaded his fingers through his slightly graying temples and pulled at the short brown strands, trying to force the suffering, torment and guilt back into the box. His name, like the premature silver in his beard and temples, fit him perfectly. Mr. Doom and Gloom himself. No doubt about it, Gray was a hot mess and he knew it.

He just didn't know how to fix himself.

At this point, he didn't believe he could. Nothing had worked. Not the counselors or their forced therapy. Not the self-help books Zane had sent him. And certainly not the alcohol. Most people this low would turn to their friends, but he didn't have any left.

Well, except for Zane. And they barely talked anymore. Thank Christ Zane had left when he did and never got sucked into ghost ops like Gray had.

His entire team had been killed down in South America when a mission went sideways and there was nothing Gray could've done to save them. The fact he'd survived himself had been a miracle. Now he viewed it as a curse.

Gray hated his life, how he was pissing it away, still unable to cope with the guilt and depression. Survivor's guilt, his therapist had called it. Gray called it the worst sort of hell. He'd failed his brothers, the men who had been his closest friends, and witnessed the horror that had accompanied their deaths.

On nights like these, he wanted nothing more than to leave this world and join his brothers in Valhalla.

But Gray's problem was he didn't have it in his DNA to give up. He was a tenacious sonofabitch. However, the sad truth was, he'd lost hope a long time ago. With no family left either, his world seemed to be growing more dark and more lonely. At least losing his parents hadn't been a shock. They'd had him when they were older and passed away peacefully five years ago, one right after the other. It had been far too long since he'd visited their graves back in Tennessee. Just another pound of guilt to weigh down his fractured, barely beating heart.

Breathing in the rain-scented air, Gray knew he was teetering on the edge, one slippery step away from hitting rock bottom. And the idea of leaving all this behind once and for all began to sound better and better. Maybe after another beer, he'd find the guts to finally do something about it.

Pushing his large frame up from the lawn chair, he decided to get that sixth beer and see where it would lead him. He shoved the screen door open and it squeaked on its hinges before slamming shut behind him. The trailer was small and slowly falling apart because Gray couldn't be bothered with fixing anything. He just didn't care anymore.

Well, that wasn't entirely true. He cared about the last friend he had left—Zane "Banshee" Hawkins. They'd hit it off right away during BUD/S and that had only been the beginning. Going through the grueling training bonded them in a way he'd never experienced before. Through all the ups and downs, they'd had each other's backs and looked out for each other in every way. Being a SEAL created a brotherhood that others couldn't understand unless they wore the Trident.

After cracking open a fresh beer, he took a long swig then set it on the edge of the counter. His gaze landed on his cell phone sitting there and he reached for it, on the verge of calling Zane...then let his hand drop back down to his side again.

Asking for help had never been his strong suit. Besides, unlike him, his friend had a life, a great intelligence job and probably a girlfriend or two. Despite the prevailing stereotype men with his higher-than-average IQ and crazy talent for hacking carried, Zane never had a problem with the ladies.

Not that Gray did, either, but that was back in his heyday. Before everything went to shit. Since losing his team a year ago, the last thing on his mind was getting laid. Now he was more concerned about trying to make it through the day and avoid the nightmares that inevitably came nearly every night.

The night terrors were another reason he hadn't brought a woman home. The humiliation of waking them both up in the middle of the night with his screams was more than he could stomach.

Raking a hand through his military-short brown hair, Gray squeezed his eyes shut and was immediately assaulted by images of his teammates being hunted down in that goddamn jungle. Shutting them down before the memories became too intense, he absently rubbed the scar on his arm again and his gaze fell on the framed picture of his team.

Grabbing the beer, he walked over to the bookshelf and stared at his fallen brothers. They'd been part of Gold Squadron, referred to themselves as Knights or Crusaders, and identified themselves by their unique logo, an image of a golden lion with a trident tail. They'd all gotten tattoos one drunken night and proudly sported the image somewhere. Gray's roaring lion was on his upper left biceps.

He'd added more ink not long after losing them—a bonefrog. The black skeletal frog on his back shoulder was a sacred and iconic image in the SEAL teams and honored those SEALs who made the ultimate sacrifice in defense of country and freedom.

What a crazy, dysfunctional yet perfectly well-oiled machine they'd been. Always joking around and having fun when they weren't out taking down the bad guys and helping make the world a safer place.

Christ, he missed them.

"Fuck," he hissed. The loss hit him like a freight train all over again and no matter how much time passed, it never felt like it was getting any better or easing. And tonight, the guilt and nightmares were becoming too damn much to bear.

Gray downed the rest of his beer, still not even feeling a buzz, and looked up in the mirror hanging on the wall. His golden amber eyes were haunted. Almost supernatural in the dim glow of the lamp.

His SEAL nickname had been Demon because he'd been so obsessed with the Dodge Demon that he wouldn't shut up about it. It was his dream machine, and he could rattle off every fact about the muscle car. Still loved the damn thing, but owning one was a pipe dream. But over time, the moniker took on a deeper meaning. His teammates had always joked that he should breach every building first because his glowing amber eyes would scare the shit out of their enemies. Maybe they'd think he was possessed and take off before he consumed their very souls.

Sometimes, Gray did feel possessed. Held by a memory that wouldn't release its claws on his own soul.

Gray downed the rest of his beer, set the bottle on an end table and suddenly knew what he was going to do. And live or die, he'd accept the consequences.

Swiping up the key to his motorcycle, he walked outside, splashed through puddles and pulled the tarp off his Kawasaki Ninja. He needed to exorcize the demons torturing him tonight and what better way to do that than take a demon ride?

He'd done it before, but not after six beers and during a rainstorm. It seemed fitting, though, since the outside weather matched his inner turmoil. And, at this point, the truth was he didn't fucking care anymore.

Habit had him put his helmet on, but he didn't secure the strap as he started the bike and blinked through the falling rain. The drops stuck to his lashes, quickly soaking through his t-shirt, and he revved the engine before blasting away into the darkness, spraying up rocks and dirt in his wake.

It was hard to see, but the rain seemed to be easing up as he made his way over to nearby Tuna Canyon Road. Among the many narrow canyon roads in the Santa Monica Mountains, Tuna Canyon was infamous for its narrowness and difficult sharp turns. Locals said it was the place where Satan and his twenty-nine virgins lived. Whatever the hell that meant.

Nowadays, the younger generation who drove down the treacherous one-way street as fast as possible called it "canyon carving." But a demon ride was an entirely different animal, its basic requirements that it took place at night and in total darkness.

Gray flipped his headlights off, revved the engine then accelerated, damn near ripping the asphalt off the road. His soul mourned his lost brothers, and no amount of danger or speed would end his suffering. But it might possibly end him and, at that moment, he hoped it did.

He had seventy turns to take in the next four miles, almost fifteen hundred feet above sea level, and in total blackness. The one-way road was precarious enough in the daylight with its twists, turns, steep drop-offs and lack of guard rails. But add in the wet road, and that took it to a whole new level of danger.

Suicide, really. But tonight he had a death wish. So whatever happened in the next four miles before he hit the Pacific Coast Highway was his destiny.

Tearing blindly around one curve after another, tilting the bike precariously, Gray drove far faster than anyone in their right mind would. But it had been a long time since he'd had a clear head and, hell, he probably had always been a little mad.

The melancholy moon above, barely a sliver, offered him the faintest light as he cruised down the steep, winding hill far too fast. A rock wall towered high on his right and a sheer drop with no guard rail teased his left. A sharp hairpin turn was coming up fast and Gray leaned to the side, so low he nearly skimmed the ground with his knee. A sharp rock bounced up and hit his face, but he welcomed the sting.

More than halfway through the ride, he pushed harder and each time he hit a brief straightaway, he increased his speed. Maybe he was just punishing himself for being the only one who survived the massacre that happened in that Colombian jungle. Because if he truly wanted to end things, he could simply drive off the edge of the mountain.

Perhaps the possibility that Gray might still have something left to live for, a reason why he hadn't died beside his brothers, burned in the back of his mind. Did he still have a purpose, some reason why he'd been spared?

Gray had never been one to believe in signs, but right now he needed one. Desperately.

Careening down the side of the mountain, he glanced up and asked for guidance. For an answer. For enlightenment. For fucking anything.

Then he went flying around another sharp curve and his tires hit a patch of wet sand mixed with some loose rock. The Kawasaki lost traction and slid onto its side, dragging Gray beneath it and across the road.

Sparks flew, his helmet flew and the pavement came up to crack against his skull.

******

Gray didn't know if he was alive or dead.

For a long moment, he laid on his back as a light rain sprinkled down around him, coating his face with a fine, wet mist.

"Is that him?" a deep voice asked.

"Yeah, that's Demon."

"You said he could be moody. I don't recall you mentioning anything about being batshit crazy," another voice commented dryly.

Gray's eyes fluttered open and he squinted through the haze of drizzle and darkness. A group of men stood there, staring down at him. They each wore a tactical neck gaiter, so Gray couldn't see any features below their eyes.

"Who are you?" he rasped, pushing up onto an elbow. A sharp pain sliced down his left side where he'd wiped out and he grimaced.

"You wanna die?" a man with gray eyes asked.

Do I?

"Because we'll grant your wish."

No, Gray decided. Maybe he wasn't ready to leave this Earth yet. And maybe these men were the answer he'd been searching for.

Without warning, the man with the black eyes tossed a bag over his head.

Shit. Maybe not.

Chapter Twenty-Two

The day of Tanner's funeral wasn't easy, and Ryland was grateful to have Harper by his side. He wished she could stay there forever. But their new plan would prohibit that. Ryland still needed to tell her and he wasn't looking forward to it. He didn't want to leave her but, at the same time, how could he possibly ask her to do what they were about to do?

It wasn't fair to ask her to make that kind of sacrifice.

Ryland was grateful for the opportunity to give his friend a proper goodbye and burial. The rest of the team was there and they mourned the loss of their fellow teammate together. In the back of his mind, Ryland tried to squash the nagging suspicion that one of these people he'd been working so closely with could possibly be responsible. It made his stomach turn.

Before the ceremony concluded, Ryland walked up to the coffin and pounded his Trident pin into the wood. Then he gave his friend a final, sharp salute. When he returned to Harper's side, she slid her hand in his and squeezed.

Banshee followed suit, walked up, pushed his pin into the wood and gave it one, sharp pound with his fist. It was a sign of utmost respect and honor for their fallen SEAL brother.

Watching Banshee salute the casket, Ryland realized it was getting harder and harder for him to figure out who he could trust. But Banshee just moved up on his short list of trustworthy people after doing that.

Maybe he was just being paranoid. But Selma and his father had gotten into his head.

Thank God for Harper. She was the one constant in his life right now and he was beginning to depend on her like he'd never depended on anyone before. That's why tonight was going to be so damn hard. Because he had to explain the plan to her and it was going to kill him. It meant they would have to say goodbye. And right now he'd rather rip his heart out than leave her.

******

It had been a rough day and after Tanner's funeral, the team had gone out to celebrate his life with dinner and drinks. Harper genuinely liked Ryland's team. Even the dark and broody Saint who had a wicked sarcastic streak that made her laugh.

They also just added Grayson Ellis to their team. Ryland told her they'd found the former SEAL lying on his back in the rain after wiping out on a suicidal run down the side of a mountain. Bringing him onboard made her nervous because she needed to know Ryland could rely on his team. Already, they were calling the new guy "Gloom and Doom" which didn't make her feel any better than when they were calling him Demon.

Ryland told her Gray was getting organized in L.A. and would be joining the team tomorrow morning on the jet.

That meant one very big thing: Ex Nihilo was flying off again and Harper had a funny feeling there wasn't a seat waiting for her. She couldn't pinpoint the reason exactly because she knew Ryland wouldn't leave her high and dry. He'd vowed to protect her.

But something felt off.

For whatever reason, Harper had the uncanny feeling this could be their last night together. Maybe because she could read Ryland so well now and something had changed after he and his team had a private meeting right before Tanner's funeral. She'd backed off, let them talk alone together, and now doubts assailed her.

Maybe she was just being paranoid. Even though she refused to accept this was their last night together, she wasn't going to waste a second.

The moment they returned to the hotel, clothes dropped to the floor and they backed over to the bed, kissing and desperate. Unable to get enough of each other. So many emotions filled Harper and she funneled them into the moment. As they fell onto the bed, Harper wound her arms around Ryland's neck, pulling him closer and savoring the feel of his warm skin against hers.

Ryland lit a fire inside of her. One that not only set her body ablaze, but also ignited her desire to help him stop The Agency. She wanted to be there by his side, and knowing he could end up like Tanner...

She couldn't think about that right now. Instead, she gave herself over to him completely, the man who had rescued her more than once and who she'd fallen in love with so deeply, so thoroughly, that it left her in a tailspin.

Desperation fueled them and there was nothing slow or tender about their coupling. An intense, fierce need drove them. Harper arched up against Ryland's hand when he cupped her center and she dropped her head back and moaned as he slid his fingers inside her wet core. Using his thumb to circle her clit, he had her writhing and crying out his name in no time.

Pleasure rolled through her and her hips undulated against his hand as he propelled her to new heights. Her release was intense and she started to sink into the bed when Ryland turned her over, hoisted her hips up off the bed and nudged her legs further apart.

Up on her hands and knees, breathing hard, Harper let her cheek drop against the sheet. Behind her, Ryland teased his tip along her wet slit then sank his cock deep with one fast, hard thrust.

"Oh, God!" Harper fisted the sheets as he began to pound into her. Hips pistoning, rhythm relentless, their bodies slapped together. Ryland reached around and began to strum her clit with his fingers, plunging in and out of her body.

"Fuck, Harper. You feel so good."

Slamming her ass back against him, she fell into the fast rhythm he set, matching his frantic strokes. "So do you. God, Ryland, you fill me up so much."

Her body squeezed around him, propelling them both toward orgasm, but he waited for her to come first. Everything tensed then released in multiple spasms that rocked her world. With a sharp cry, she dug her nails into the mattress and screamed into the blanket, letting the waves of release wash over her.

His orgasm hit him a moment later and he groaned through it, hips pumping then slowing down as a tremor rocked through his big body. Panting hard, he leaned over her and she felt him press a kiss to her spine. "I love you," he rasped.

When he slid out of her body, she immediately felt the loss and she dropped down with a half-sob. Gently flipping her over, Ryland's gaze met hers and Harper cupped his stubbled jaw. "I love you, too," she whispered, then kissed him with every ounce of love flowing through her.

And, once again, Harper had the horrible premonition that he was about to leave her.

******

The emotional day had been draining and exhausting. After taking Harper hard and fast, needing the release and solace only she could provide, Ryland wrapped his arms around her and they drifted off to sleep. A few hours later, he woke up and couldn't bear the thought of walking away from her.

Breathing her scent in deeply, Ryland buried his face in her neck and began kissing her soft skin. She awoke and he moved between her legs, waking her fully with his mouth, his hands and finally his cock.

On some level, he knew this would be it. Their last time together until The Agency was toppled and defeated. What had been fast and frenzied earlier turned into slow and sensual. Harper's legs dropped open, welcoming him, and he teased her for several long, torturous minutes before angling her hips and sinking home.

Ryland positioned her just right then began a slow, steady drag in and out of her soaked pussy. He wanted to take his time and hit her sweet spot over and over again. Make sure they didn't rush because he wanted to savor it all. Remember the feel of connecting with her physically and emotionally.

"Oh, fuck," he groaned, trying not to speed up, but gritting his teeth as the tension at the base of his spine began to build.

"Faster," Harper urged, digging her nails into his flexing ass, trying to pull him deeper.

If she wanted faster, he wasn't going to say no. Ryland picked up his pace and a minute later, they both broke at exactly the same moment. They flew over the precipice together, joined in every way, then floated back down to reality.

Ryland dotted light kisses along Harper's collarbone. "I…" he licked the hollow, "…love…" swirled his tongue, "…you…"

He'd never told any woman those words except his mother and sister. And that had been a very long time ago. He may have only known Harper a short time, but he knew what he felt for her. It was undeniable and incredible. Even more spiritual than catching a tube. Because he knew without a doubt that Harper had barreled him. One-hundred and ten percent.

"I—" Her voice caught and she squeezed her eyes shut.

"What?" Ryland traced a finger along her jaw then pressed a kiss to her lips. "Tell me, sweetheart. What're you thinking?"

"I know you guys came up with some sort of plan. But you haven't told me yet, and that worries me." She hesitated then asked, "You're leaving, aren't you?"

He'd been dreading this moment and seeing her tear-bright eyes killed him. Heaving out a sigh, he said, "Harper, I need you to understand the gravity of what we're planning to do. We're setting up our base ops in a small, remote town about halfway up the coast. The rules suck, but make sense: burner phones only, and only when absolutely necessary; no credit cards, only cash; and no talking to anyone in our past, including family and friends."

She frowned, hooking her finger in his silver chain. "Wherever you go, I want to go, too."

"There's more," he said hesitantly. "It's not going to be easy to find and eliminate our targets while constantly looking over our shoulder as they're simultaneously hunting us down. So we made a decision."

He locked gazes with her.

"Tomorrow morning, the team is boarding a private plane. The flight plan will say we're heading to Mexico, but halfway there, we're going to jump out of the plane before crashing it in a remote desert location. The world will think we died. No survivors. It's the only way to keep the people we love safe. Otherwise, The Agency could use them to try to track us down."

Harper's jaw dropped and she released the necklace. "You're going to fake your deaths so they stop pursuing you?"

Ryland nodded, brushing a strand of golden hair back off her face. "And then we're going to hunt down every single bastard behind Tanner's death and eliminate them one by one."

She considered his words then said, "I want to go with you."

"I can't ask that of you. Your sister would be devastated."

"What about your sister?" Harper prodded.

Ryland scrubbed a hand over his jaw. "That's complicated."

"What do you mean?"

"I haven't told you anything about Addie yet because we're not on the best of terms right now." Ryland considered his next words carefully and Harper waited patiently for him to continue. "My older sister takes after our mother."

"Meaning?"

"She's a world-class thief. Remember when you mentioned my lockpicking skills?"

Harper nodded.

"Courtesy of good ol' mom. And my middle name?"

"Vincenzo."

"Named after Vincenzo Peruggia, arguably the greatest art thief of the 20th century."

"What made him so good?"

"He managed to steal the Mona Lisa from the Louvre."

"Seriously? How?"

"That's the funny part. He worked there and didn't have any kind of elaborate plan. Just hid in the museum one night, took the painting off the wall, put it under his jacket and walked out. Got caught when he tried to sell it two years later."

"I assume he went to prison."

"Just for a year. Then he served in the Italian Army

during World War I and now is considered a hero there."

"That's crazy."

"My mom's penchant for stealing is one of the reasons she and my dad divorced. Problem is she was so damn good at it. And, of course, she taught Addie everything she knew. So, I guess you could say my sister is carrying on her legacy."

"I'd like to meet her," Harper said with no hesitation. "After we defeat The Agency."

We. She made it sound like she was staying with him. Was that even a possibility? He couldn't think about it. "Even though she's a thief?" Ryland asked, voice skeptical.

"Sure, why not? You're an assassin and I think we get along pretty well," she teased.

The corner of Ryland's mouth edged up. "God, what am I going to do without you?"

"We don't have to worry about that because I'm coming with you."

"Harper..." But hope lit his heart. Maybe—just maybe—she could come. But it was asking so much of her. Even so, he felt his resolve crumbling because he wanted it just as badly as she did.

"I've made up my mind."

Stubborn, little thing. He released a pent-up breath, caving to her. And to his own selfish wants and desires. "You have to be sure. And I'm talking one-hundred and ten percent fucking positive because there's no going back. You understand it means you would have to die with the rest of us?"

"I understand." She clutched his hand. "I'd like to say goodbye to Savannah, though. If that's possible."

His heart stuttered. She was fucking choosing him. Choosing a future together despite the danger. A warmth spread through Ryland's chest and he laced his fingers through hers. "You'll stay with me?" When was the last time someone had chosen him? His heart clenched.

Never.

She tilted her head and gave him a small smile. "You think you can just fake your own death and get rid of me? No way, mister. I'm not letting you go that easily."

"I don't want to get rid of you, sweetheart. But I also can't ask you to give up a normal life and go into hiding with us for God knows how long."

"You're right. You don't have to ask because I'll gladly do it. As long as Savannah knows I'm okay, that's all I care about."

For a moment, Ryland mulled over her words,

considering every angle. The Agency wanted Ex Nihilo dead. And once that happened, or they believed it had happened, they would have no need for Harper, her sister, or any of their family and friends.

Ryland knew he should send Harper home. Let her go. But the self-serving bastard inside him wanted to keep her close and never let her go. And what better way to do that than to make it permanent? Make it forever. If she was going to take a leap of faith, then so would he.

He could make Harper his wife. Something that he'd been thinking about since the moment she started breathing again after he pulled her out of the water. Because even though he was aware that he was doing the same thing his father had done years ago, Ryland wanted to handle it differently.

"I'm thinking some things right now," he said slowly. "Maybe crazy things."

"I'm in," Harper said with zero hesitation.

"You don't even know what I'm going to say."

"If it involves you and me, I'm saying yes."

He lifted her hand and asked, "What about if it involves you, me and forever?"

"Forever?" she echoed.

Ryland pressed a kiss to the ring finger of her left

hand. "Yeah, forever."

"I'd say the forever stories are the best ones. And I'd like a forever story with you, Ryland."

Holy shit, she's saying yes. Ryland's throat closed as he slid off the bed, dropped down onto his knee and pulled her closer.

"I'm going to do this right. Or, at least semi-right since we're both naked and it's the middle of the night."

Her mouth edged up and Ryland grasped her hand tightly in his.

"Harper Lane Grant, I've never felt a connection this intense to anyone before in my life. From the first day we met, I knew there was something different about you. The chemistry was off the charts, but it was another, deeper feeling that drew me to you. Like I'd found my other half. As cheesy as it sounds, it's true. Almost losing you scared the shit out me, sweetheart. Our time together is too precious and I don't want to spend another second away from you. So, if you'll have me, I promise to keep you close and safe. I'll guard you with my life and love you til my last breath. Harper, will you marry me?"

"Yes," she breathed, then pulled him up and into bed again. "A thousand times yes."

Their mouths met in a long, sensual kiss, sealing the deal, and Ryland felt like the luckiest man in the world.

Epilogue

The next morning, Ryland and Harper woke up extra early and went down to the courthouse. They were legally declared man and wife thirty minutes later. Back outside on the sunny steps, Ryland spun his wife in a circle then kissed her thoroughly.

"Love you, Mrs. Mills," he said.

Harper laughed and her aqua eyes lit up with mischief. "Are we completely insane?"

"Probably. But isn't that half the fun?"

She smirked then kissed him again. "I love you, Mr. Mills. And I'm looking forward to starting our lives together. Even if we'll be in hiding for an indeterminate amount of time."

"As long as the team gives us some privacy because as newlyweds, I plan to spend every spare moment in bed with you."

He nipped her ear and she yelped. "You're so bad."

After a quick stop at the jewelry store where they bought a couple of simple gold bands, they drove straight to the restaurant so Harper could say goodbye to her sister. It was an emotional scene. They'd already spoken earlier and Harper had explained the situation on the way over to the courthouse. Taking Savannah into their confidence might be a risky move, but Harper had assured him she wouldn't tell a soul. Especially not if it risked all of their lives.

Everything was happening so fast and Ryland stepped away to give them some privacy. But Savannah told him to stay. After all, they were family now. She seemed genuinely happy for them and started crying when Harper reminded her of their flight. They had to leave, but the sisters were holding each other, and Ryland felt a stab of guilt for putting them through this.

"We'll still be able to talk." Harper gave her sister a final hug. "Just use a burner."

Savannah clutched the bag of disposable phones tightly to her chest and swiped at her watery eyes. "I will."

"I'll call you tonight when we're safely in—"

Harper glanced over at Ryland and he shrugged his shoulders. "Well, when we're wherever we're going."

"You better buy her a damn big diamond for going through all this," Savannah mumbled to her new brother-in-law.

"Oh, I will," Ryland assured her. He hesitated then pulled an envelope out of his pocket and handed it to Savannah. Harper had told him about the restaurant and the financial trouble her sister was in and he had plenty of money stashed. Helping her out and making sure the sisters could achieve their dream was the least he could do.

"What's this?"

"Open it," Harper encouraged her.

Savannah's brow creased as she tore the envelope open and looked down at the thick wad of cash with wide eyes.

"I'm sorry we can't be here to help with the rest of the renovation," Harper said.

"But that should cover any issues you run into," Ryland finished.

"Oh, my God, I can't accept this."

"Of course, you can. We're family now, right?" Ryland slid his arm around Harper, pulling her close.

"Seriously?" Savannah's eyes flooded with tears.

"Get Charlie's Place up and running, and I'll get your sister back home as soon as I possibly can," Ryland told her.

"Thank you," Savannah murmured and sniffled softly. Then Harper stepped over and they hugged hard one last time.

"Take good care of Betty," Harper reminded her.

"I will," Savannah promised.

Harper hesitated, looking around the restaurant. "You'll be okay?"

"Go," Savannah told her. "And thank you. I'll talk to you soon, right?"

"Yeah, soon. Love you, sis."

"Love you, too."

******

After the emotional goodbye, Ryland and Harper headed to the private airstrip. The team was already waiting and when they saw Harper, they all paused.

"Why is she here?" Saint demanded, exhaling a cloud of smoke through his nostrils. He took another long drag of his cigarette then flicked the butt away.

Ryland and Harper lifted their hands and flashed their wedding bands. "My wife goes where I go."

"Are you fucking kidding me?" Banshee exclaimed, his eyes lighting up behind his glasses. "Dude, congratulations!"

"Oh, my God!" Bruja cried and ran over to give them both a big hug. "I'm so happy for you both."

Pharaoh raised a brow then muttered his congratulations. He didn't look too surprised.

Gray Ellis stood off to the side and Ryland waved him over. "Demon, this is Harper. My wife."

"Nice to meet you," Harper said and shook the big man's hand. "Can I call you something other than Demon, though? Sorry, but it kind of freaks me out."

"Gray," he told her. His deep voice was scratchy and his unusual golden eyes glinted like twin amber stones.

"That's a much better name than Demon," she said and, for the first time since he'd agreed to be a part of their team, Gray's mouth edged up in the faintest hint of a smile, though it didn't reach his eyes.

Harper's comment also got Ryland thinking and the moment everyone was seated and the plane began taxiing over to the runway, he said, "Now that we're going deep undercover, I need to know I can trust you guys fully."

"You don't trust your team?" Pharaoh asked, gray eyes narrowing.

"I don't know my team. We've been going by codenames and were ordered not to spend time together outside of work. Am I the only one who thought that was a little strange?"

"Normally teams are encouraged to bond," Banshee agreed.

"Exactly," Ryland said. "I need to know I can trust each one of you. Keeping Harper safe and bringing down The Agency are my number one priorities. I'm not going to lie—Selma and my dad planted seeds of doubt."

"Your dad did, too?" Pharaoh asked.

"They both claimed one of us is a traitor. A mole."

Everyone straightened up, listening closely.

"I need to put my mind at ease, so I'm asking everyone to share their real name and background. Hell, Tanner told me after knowing me for an hour. Yet none of you ever revealed anything."

"Because we were ordered not to," Saint said.

"It's totally suspect," Bruja agreed. "Yeah, I'd like to know, too."

Ryland looked over the group. "I'll go first. If you didn't already figure it out, my name is Ryland Mills and

I'm a former Navy SEAL."

"Red Squadron?" Banshee asked.

Ryland nodded and flashed the ink on his forearm depicting the tomahawk and red and black feathers. "Never was much of a secret."

"That's because you boys mark yourselves all up," Bruja said. "Banshee, you mentioned you and Demon were briefly on the same team. I would've sworn you were military intelligence until you gave a 'hooyah' and then pounded your Trident into Tanner's casket."

"We were both Knights for a short while."

"Gold Squadron," Gray clarified without a trace of emotion.

"Then I was recruited over to Black Squadron."

"Oh, shit," Ryland murmured, tipping his head Banshee's way in a silent nod of recognition. Of all the color-coded squadrons, Black Squadron was the ultra-secretive arm of DEVGRU, responsible for intelligence, reconnaissance, and surveillance.

"Real name?" Bruja asked, leaning forward.

"Zane Hawkins. What about you?"

"Well, you already know I'm former Army. And my real name is Inda Diaz. To be honest, I'm getting a little tired of being called a witch."

308

"But you're a beguiling witch," Zane said, and she grinned, rolling her eyes.

"Save your charm for someone who cares," she told him, and he chuckled.

No one focused on Gray because they already knew his story from Zane.

"Saint?" Ryland asked.

"My name is Nik Valentine."

"Nik Valentine?" Inda repeated dubiously. "That sounds made up."

"It's the name I choose to go by. My birth name is Nikolai Vasilevsky."

"Ha! I knew you were Russian," Ryland exclaimed, pointing a finger at him.

"I claim no kin," Nik stated.

"How did you get hired by a U.S. government agency when you're not even American?" Zane prodded.

"I am an American, you asshole," Nik said. "I left Russia years ago and became a citizen."

"And you worked for Russian Intelligence?" Pharaoh asked.

Nik leaned back in his seat and sent a defiant look

to everyone. "Let's be clear that I don't talk about my past. But since Rip—excuse me, *Ryland*—is having trust issues, I'll tell you once and don't ever fucking ask me again."

Everyone seemed to be waiting with bated breath and Ryland's gaze dipped to the black ink along Nik's knuckles, hands and forearms. He recognized some of the symbols—tattoos always told a story—and Nik had already revealed he'd spent time in a Russian prison where every inmate was marked and every drop of ink held meaning from time served to crimes committed.

"I worked for the Federal Security Service and was sent deep undercover in the Bratva. I barely made it out alive. If you didn't already know, the Russian mob are a bunch of cocksuckers. But, again, let me be crystal clear. I don't talk about it, so don't ask me any more fucking questions."

He speared them all with a look that clearly stated he was done sharing.

Damn, how deeply undercover had he been willing to go? Ryland wondered. Between working for the FSS and the Bratva, it was a wonder Nik had survived those two monsters.

"Alrighty then," Bruja said, and everyone looked at Pharaoh who was the last to share his story.

"Braxton Graves, former Delta Force commander.

Spec ops."

"I knew it!" Ryland exclaimed.

"Same!" Zane said and the two slapped hands and bumped knuckles.

"Why would you think he was Delta Force?" Harper asked.

"Because he reeks of spec ops and has that calm, cool control about him at all times. Like nothing can ruffle the dude's feathers," Ryland answered.

"It's my job to stay calm, especially when I'm leading my team," Braxton stated. "And you can call me Brax."

With all of that intel now on the table, Ryland felt a little better. In order for this plan to work, he had to trust every one of them with his life. And now Harper's, too.

"No offense, Rip, but the one person I had trouble trusting was your father," Inda commented. "And you do realize you're about to pull the same stunt he did. We all are."

"Yeah." He didn't want to get into that part of the plan further because he'd already decided he was going to send Addie an encrypted message that only she would understand, assuring her he was fine. There was no way he would let her mourn for him when he was still alive. He wasn't his father. "What triggered your mistrust?"

Ryland met Inda's caramel eyes, curious. Because he felt the same damn way.

"It all seemed a little too convenient. Him warning you and still being alive. I don't know. I got weird vibes."

Yeah, same.

"Let's gear up," Pharaoh ordered, reminding his team they were about to jump out of an airplane.

As the others began to prepare for the jump, Ryland reached around and, for the first time in ten years, removed the silver chain hanging around his neck. Staring down at his father's cross in his palm, an array of emotions battered through him. But he didn't have time to think about that right now. He set it down on the seat, almost reverently, and a wave of sadness washed over him. Now the cross would be nothing more than evidence recovered. A charred reminder of what could've been when it came to the relationship he and his father had.

"You okay?" Harper asked softly.

"I will be," he said and forced a smile. "What about you, sweetheart? Ready to jump?"

Harper sucked in a deep breath and held out her hand. "Does this answer your question?"

It was shaking. Ryland grabbed it and squeezed. "I've got you. Always."

"You're sure we can trust your pilot?" Nik asked, glancing toward the cockpit.

"No doubt about it," Braxton answered. "Hunter is a close friend and saved my ass more than once on a mission."

Ryland hadn't met their pilot yet, but if Braxton trusted him, he knew the pilot was damn good.

As they began to check their chutes and prepare for the jump, Ryland pressed a kiss to Harper's forehead. "I'm sorry to be taking you away from home—"

"You're my home now, Ryland." Harper gave him a brave smile. But when her gaze moved over to the rest of the team, preparing for the skydive, her smile wavered.

Her nerves were increasing, so he kissed her again, this time on the lips, slowly and thoroughly. A couple of cat calls filled the air, but he ignored them. He wanted to help her relax and while he'd jumped out of a plane hundreds of times, this was Harper's first jump.

"You're going to be in my arms the entire way down, okay?"

His wife gave another brave nod and he helped her step into the harness. After checking, double-checking and triple-checking all the buckles, he slipped his equipment on and connected them together. A quick glance down at his watch told him it was go-time.

They all lined up near the door, waiting for the pilot to join them.

Beside them, Nik fidgeted with a strap, shifting his weight from one booted foot to the other. "It's been a while," he murmured around the unlit cigarette clamped between his teeth. It was the first time Ryland had ever seen the former Russian spy look nervous.

"Just like riding a bike," Ryland said and slapped his back.

The cockpit door swung open and a tall, slim woman with reddish-brown hair swept back in a low ponytail walked out. "Let's jump," she said, sliding her parachute on.

"Everyone, this is Hunter 'Pyro' McGrath," Braxton said. "A former Navy fighter pilot."

"Hooyah!" both Ryland and Zane called out.

"Hooyah!" Hunter called back.

"Pyro?" Nik asked, cocking a dark brow.

"Yeah, well, I may have *accidentally* set the base's airfield in Kabul on fire. Oops." She shrugged a non-repentant shoulder. "It really wasn't my fault. Not entirely, anyway. And no smoking on my plane."

"It's not lit," Nik growled. "And aren't we about to crash this bitch?"

"Don't remind me," she said with a soft sigh. "The things I do for you, Brax."

Ryland smothered a smirk. He hadn't expected a woman pilot and he glanced from her over to Braxton. *Hmm.* He wondered what their history was exactly. Musings left for another time and place.

"I owe you, Pyro," Braxton stated.

"That's an understatement."

Braxton moved to the door and when Hunter gave a nod, he opened it. The cabin filled with the whoosh of air currents and the entire plane shook.

"We've got less than five minutes before this bird is nothing more than a burning hole in the ground," Hunter stated. "Let's punch out."

"You heard her," Braxton said and motioned for Zane, the first in line, to jump. He stepped right out of the plane, quickly followed by Inda and then Gray. Zero hesitation.

Nik glanced down, squeezed his eyes shut, and grumbled a low, "Fuckit," before jumping out.

Ryland moved them up and Harper gasped as he positioned her in front of the open door.

"I've got you, sweetheart," he promised. "Ready?"

"Yes…no!"

Pressing a quick kiss to her temple, Ryland stepped out into thin air and Harper squealed. All sound seemed to be sucked away as they fell, and only the rush of the wind currents filled their ears. A moment later, he pulled the ripcord and they snapped upright.

As they floated down to Earth, he marveled at the peace and serenity so high up. It was time to move forward with their mission and that meant focusing on the present and letting go of the past.

And, most importantly, keeping Harper safe and close by his side.

The ground grew closer and Ryland focused on the plane which had become a dot in the distance. It would be crashing any second now and they would all be officially declared dead.

"Legs up," Ryland reminded her as they came in for a landing. His boots hit the ground hard and he guided them to a stop as smoothly as possible. Once Harper was standing, he unbuckled their suits. "You did so great. I'm so damn proud of you."

They shared a quick kiss and he started gathering the parachute blowing out behind him. The desert ground seemed to momentarily shake and, in the distance, flames and smoke rose up into the blue sky. Now they were officially ghosts.

It was a strange feeling. But they needed to be one

step ahead of The Agency and if they were assumed dead, Ryland and his team would have the upper hand. Then they could sneak in like wraiths and bring everyone on their list down.

Their enemies wouldn't know they were coming or what hit them.

As Braxton and Hunter touched down, the rest of the team gathered their chutes and prepared to jump into the waiting SUV that Hunter had set up for their quick evac.

In the meantime, Ryland turned to Harper and yanked her into his arms.

"Maybe it's selfish, but I'm really glad you're here with me."

"There's nowhere else I'd rather be," she murmured. "Who knew my surfer neighbor would turn out to be a former SEAL who would involve me in the adventure of a lifetime?"

"And now I'm your husband." He searched her face for some sign of regret. But there wasn't any.

She grinned up at him, her aqua eyes glimmering in the sun like jewels. "Wherever our future leads, I'm all in, Mr. Mills."

Ryland's mouth edged up and he cupped her face, pressed his forehead against hers and whispered, "Me, too, Mrs. Mills."

Nearby, the team stood waiting by the SUV and watched the black smoke rise in the distance. It was strange. Even though they were officially dead to the world, Ryland had never felt more alive in his entire life.

And that was all thanks to the beautiful woman standing by his side.

His love, his wife and his forever.

I hope you enjoyed book one of my Force Protection Delta series because the adventure and intrigue are just beginning. Up next, find out who helps Gray put his broken pieces back together. Happy Reading!

Acknowledgment

Writing book one of a new series is always a challenge and I can't thank my amazing editor Michelle enough for getting me to where I needed to be. I tend to write fast and worry about certain details later. Luckily, she finds those necessary details and missed opportunities where I can improve. Plus, we always have a blast picking out muses for the characters. Her knowledge of hot male models on Insta is unmatched! So, thank you, my friend—so very much! You make this journey so much more fun than I ever imagined it could be!

About the Author

A Midwest girl at heart, Charissa has lived in Boston and Los Angeles and finally returned to her hometown of Toledo, Ohio. She's an avid coffee drinker, animal lover and was named after a romance heroine. Horror movies and steamy, action-packed romance novels keep her up late at night (and probably too much caffeine). She's also written over 15 screenplays, several even produced, and despite a dreary dating history, she still believes in love at first sight.

Don't Miss Out!

To be notified of upcoming releases, news, sneak peeks and contests, come join my reading crew:
https://www.facebook.com/groups/1506114033137424

And if you enjoy steamy romantic suspense, don't forget to claim your free story, "Blue Squadron Pirates," the prequel to Project Phoenix, here:
https://BookHip.com/NLVKTAL

It's only available for readers who sign up for my VIP mailing list! You can sign up over at
www.charissagracyk.com

If you love my stories and would like free advanced copies of my books, I'm still building my ARC team and would love to have you! Just message me on my Facebook page, Charissa Gracyk, Author, or at charissagracyk@gmail.com.

Also By Charissa Gracyk

Fortune Seekers

Brighter Than Gold (Fortune Seekers Book 1)

The Brilliance of You (Fortune Seekers Book 2)

Dazzled By You (Fortune Seekers Book 3)

A Million Sparks (Fortune Seekers Book 4)

**Each book in this steamy, action-packed, romantic adventure series can be read as a standalone.

Project Phoenix

Reactivated: Oz (Project Phoenix Book1)

Reactivated: Dom (Project Phoenix Book 2)

Reactivated: Jericho (Project Phoenix Book 3)

Reactivated: Max (Project Phoenix Book 4)

Reactivated: Cassian (Project Phoenix Book 5)

Reactivated: Deacon (Project Phoenix Book 6)

Reactivated: Aidan (Project Phoenix Book 7)

**This is an interconnected series and each warrior finds

a happily-ever-after in his own story.

Slater Security

Operation: Dead Drop (Slater Security Book 1)

Operation: Shadow Catcher (Slater Security Book 2)

Operation: Light Storm (Slater Security Book 3)

Operation: Fire Bomb (Slater Security Book 4)

Operation: Free Fall (Slater Security Book 5)

**Each book in this steamy, action-packed, romantic adventure series can be read as a standalone.

Force Protection Delta

Ryland (Force Protection Delta Book 1)

Gray (Force Protection Delta Book 2)- Coming Soon!

**This is an interconnected series and each warrior finds a happily-ever-after in his own story.

Made in United States
Orlando, FL
21 November 2023

39264735R00200